THE TEENAGE Q&A BOOK

OTHER BOOKS BY JOSH MCDOWELL

EVIDENCE THAT DEMANDS A VERDICT
THE RESURRECTION FACTOR
HOW TO HELP YOUR CHILD SAY "NO" TO SEXUAL
  PRESSURE
WHY WAIT? *What You Need to Know about the Teen Sexuality
  Crisis*
TEENS SPEAK OUT: *What I Wish My Parents Knew about
  My Sexuality*
EVIDENCE FOR JOY: *Unlocking the Secrets of Being Loved,
  Accepted and Secure*
THE SECRET OF LOVING: *How a Lasting Intimacy Can
  Be Yours*
GIVERS, TAKERS, AND OTHER KINDS OF LOVERS
HIS IMAGE . . . MY IMAGE: *Biblical Principles for Improving
  Your Self-Image*
LOVE, DAD: *Positive Answers for Young Teens on Handling
  Sexual Pressure*

JOSH MCDOWELL AS SERIES EDITOR

Dating: Picking (and Being) a Winner
Sex: Desiring the Best
Love: Making it Last

THE
TEENAGE
Q&A
BOOK

JOSH McDOWELL
AND
BILL JONES

WORD PUBLISHING
Dallas·London·Vancouver·Melbourne

THE TEENAGE Q & A BOOK

Unless otherwise noted, all Scripture quotations are from the New American Standard Bible (NASB), © The Lockman Foundation 1960, 1962, 1963, 1968, 1971, 1973, 1975, 1977.

Library of Congress Cataloging-in-Publication Data

McDowell, Josh.
    The teenage Q & A book / Josh McDowell and Bill Jones.
        p.   cm.
    Summary: Addresses from a Christian viewpoint a number of topics of interest to teenagers, including parents, self-image, peer pressure, dating, and sex.
    ISBN 0-8499-3232-7
    1. Teenagers—Religious life—Miscellanea. 2. Christian life--Miscellanea—Juvenile literature. 3. Teenagers—Conduct of life--Miscellanea. [1. Conduct of life. 2. Christian life.
3. Adolescence.] I. Jones, Bill, 1955–   . II. Title.
III. Title: Teenage Q and A book. IV. Title: Teenage question and answer book.
BV4531.2.M23   1990
248.8'3—dc20   90-38428
                                                                      CIP
                                                                      AC

Printed in the United States of America

5 6 7 8 9 LBM 17 16 15

. . . The Scriptures are able to make you wise. And that wisdom leads to salvation through faith in Jesus Christ. All Scripture is useful for teaching and for showing people what is wrong with their lives. It is useful for correcting faults and teaching how to live right.

2 Timothy 3:15, 16 *Everyday Bible*

Acknowledgments

We readily acknowledge that this book is the result of the efforts of many people. Bill and I are indebted to the numerous youth pastors and their youth groups that gave us valuable input on the questions young people are asking. We want to thank Marcus Maranto of the Josh McDowell Ministry Research Department for his valuable contribution, Pam Key of Student Mission Impact for her untiring effort of inputing the manuscript, Dave Bellis for working through the maze of details, for structuring the book and readying the manuscript, and Al Bryant and Joey Paul of Word Publishing for their guidance and labor of love. Ultimately our thanks is to God, the ministry He has given both of us and the opportunity to share these questions and answers with parents, pastors, youth workers and young people whom we love so much.

Josh McDowell

Bill Jones

Contents

THE
TEENAGE
Q&A
BOOK

 **1** *Parents*

Q. *Why do my parents sometimes look at me like I just arrived from outer space?*

A. In a word, because you have changed. Consider your appetite. Where you once ate three meals a day (excluding vegetables of course), you now have the appetite of a giant termite consuming a week's worth of groceries in a matter of minutes without any help from your friends. Speaking of which, your parents don't routinely interact with a person dressed in black leather with orange hair and a three-carat diamond in his pierced nose.

If those two developments alone aren't enough to amaze them, what about your growth? They may be somewhat fearful that if you keep growing at the same rate you have been growing, your body might soon be as big as your mouth (from their perspective, of course). Your intelligence has also grown. You now know everything about everything.

Where you once were polite and well mannered, you now burp in public and respond to all questions with a terse, "Leave me alone." You no longer require any sleep. You go to bed at 4 A.M. and get up at 7.

If you are a guy, you never leave your room. If you are a girl, you never come out of the bathroom.

In a matter of months they have witnessed a radical transformation take place in their "little boy" or "little girl." Little wonder they sometimes look at you as if you are sort of strange. Don't worry, the same thing happened to them. It's a great time of life that everyone goes through. Parents speak of it with great memories in regard to themselves, but with fear and trembling when it comes to their own children. It's called the teenage years.

Q. *Why do my parents make such a big deal about my hair and clothes? I'm not hurting anyone, am I?*

A. Possibly. Depends on how much hair spray you used. After two or three cans of it, your spike can become a lethal weapon. If you bent over and rammed someone it might go right through them.

   Parents make a big deal about the way you look for the same reason you make a big deal about the way they look. Think about it.

   When your friends are over, why do you panic any time your parents ask permission to come out of their room? You're afraid your friends will think you have weird parents, right? You don't really care if people like your parents, as long as your friends think they are normal human beings.

   The same is true for your parents. They want their friends to think you are a "normal" teenager because they don't want them to think you are weird. To a parent, a normal teenager is a cross between Wally Cleaver (on "Leave it to Beaver," if you watch reruns) and Mary Ann (from "Gilligan's Island"). You have to remember that's the TV diet on which they grew up. The truth of the matter is a "normal" teenager *is* more like an alien than anything else your parents or their friends are used to.

Q. *Why don't my parents like any of my friends?*

A. There are probably different reasons for different friends. Usually the main reason is fear that a particular friend has been or will be a negative influence on you. They know (possibly from experience) how easy it is to pick up bad habits, and they don't want you to get into trouble. Or perhaps your parents think your friend is disrespectful. For example, take a typical phone conversation: your friend calls up and asks, with the sensitivity of a water buffalo, "Is Wild Man Willie there?" They would much rather hear a polite, "May I speak to William please? This is Mark calling."

Another reason is they might be thinking your friend isn't good enough for you. This is true especially if your friend is of the opposite sex and you want to date him or her. Perhaps the underlying reason for all of these is that your parents want the best for you and very few of your friends can measure up to their standards. This issue, like many others in your relationship with your parents, can be a reason to initiate World War III or communicate (peacefully) some strong feelings. Choose the latter and be glad your parents care for you.

Q. *My Mom and Dad are constantly lecturing me and they always begin with "Well, when I was your age. . . ." Why can't my parents understand what it's like to be a teenager today?*

A. Do you want the good news first or the bad news? Let's get the bad news out of the way first. Check out Luke 2:41–51. It's the story of Jesus just about the time He became a teenager. He somehow didn't make connections with His folks and got separated from them.

4

When His parents found Him the conversation went like this:

"And He said to them, 'Why is it that you were looking for Me? Did you not know that I had to be in My Father's house?' And they did not understand the statement which He had made to them. And He went down with them, and came to Nazareth; and He continued in subjection to them; and His mother treasured all these things in her heart" (Luke 2:49–51).

Sound familiar? Here is the bad news. If the parents of Jesus didn't understand Him, don't be surprised if yours don't understand you sometimes. Remember, your parents grew up in a different era. Your parents were probably born just about the time TV was invented! It is not easy for them to relate to your generation, but neither was it easy for their parents to relate to them. Every generation struggles to understand the next generation. But the good news is, you can respond the same way that Jesus did. As a Christian you have the power to do that. Philippians 4:13 says: "I can do all things through Him who strengthens me."

Q. It is so hard to talk to my parents. When I do, they don't listen. What does it take to communicate with them?

A. Communication is hard work. It's often easier to say nothing than to talk things out. But watch out for making excuses not to communicate: "They never listen anyway"; "We will only end up fighting"; or "They will just make fun of me."

Also avoid communication-killers. When your parents don't seem to understand, it doesn't take long to form habits that kill communication. Some of these are:

The Silent Treatment. You don't speak at all to your parents (usually to "get even" for something).

The Last Word. This can be done with anger or with controlled politeness. You have to have the last word.

I'll Just Put Up with It. You say what you think your parents want to hear, then go out secretly and do what you want anyway.

Bigger, Better, Nicer. You tell your parents how much better your friends' parents are.

Running Away. You get so frustrated that you leave the room or the house to avoid further confrontation.

Dogging Them with Dogmatism. Your conversation is full of phrases such as "You never" or "You always."

Bugging 'Em to Death. Here you believe that if you pester them long enough you can get your way (*Parents: Raising Them Properly,* pp.19, 20).

Finally, don't get frustrated and give up. Keep the lines of communication open. Even though it may feel like you are not making progress, if you try, you really are moving ahead in your relationships.

Q. My parents are too strict. They won't let me do any-thing fun. Why do they insist on so many rules?

A. God gave you the parents you have. (Thank Him, don't blame Him.) He did so for two specific reasons. One was to keep you from having fun in life and the other was to make you as miserable as possible in the process. I'm just joking, although I know at times it may seem that way.

The real reasons God gave you parents are to protect you from harm and to provide you with what's best in life.

Sounds great, doesn't it? So when are they going to get started, right? The trouble comes when what you think is fun, they see as potential harm, like staying out past midnight. And what you may see as harm, they think is the greatest thing since sliced bread, like doing homework.

So be grateful your parents care enough to follow through on their God-given responsibility, and follow through on your God-given responsibility. Ephesians 6:1 says, "Children, obey your parents in the Lord, for this is right."

Q. *My parents tell me "no" and never give me an explanation. Isn't there a law against that somewhere?*

A. The next time you want an explanation from your parents, go away for a while and cool down. Then return and ask, "Why did you say no?" Yes, it's the same question you always ask. But there is a difference this time. When you asked why in the past, your eyes were half closed, your jaw locked shut, your eyebrows furrowed, your forehead wrinkled and your ears were blowing smoke. This did not communicate, "Hey! I'm open to hearing what you have to say."

Most of the time if you ask with an attitude that says, "I want to understand your perspective and grow in wisdom," they will give you reasons. But sometimes they don't understand the reasons themselves. They only know that they "feel" uncomfortable about your doing this or that or going here or there. When that happens you just have to trust that God has put up a road block that He doesn't want you to go around.

One last thought. Be prepared for an answer that you might not agree with. You may even think it is a dumb reason. Regardless, don't blow your new-found cool. Obey them anyway.

Q. *Do I have to obey my parents if they aren't Christians?*

A. Whether or not your parents are believers has nothing to do with whether you should obey them. (Great try, though!) They deserve obedience because God placed them over you. Romans 13:1 says, "Let every person be in subjection to the governing authorities. For there is no authority except from God, and those which exist are established by God." Obedience to your parents is an expression of your obedience to God.

Q. *My parents are hypocrites. They tell me to do one thing and then they do another. It's not fair. Why should I have to do something if they aren't going to do the same?*

A. You just struck an open nerve. For example, your dad grounds you for lying and then turns around and tells your mom to say he's not home when someone calls and he doesn't want to talk with them. Or your folks tell you to go to church regardless of how tired you are, but they can lay out anytime they want. Well, welcome to life. You have just discovered the reality of the double standard.

Few people practice what they preach, but that doesn't negate the truth of God's Word. He says to obey those over you because of who you are (His child, a follower of Jesus Christ the Lord), not because of what they do or don't do.

Besides, your parents realize, painfully enough, that they aren't perfect. You don't need to help them see their faults. Try encouraging them. It will work wonders.

Q. *Whenever I ask them to do something, my parents have a one word response (No!). How can I get them, at least every once in a while, to say, "Yes"?*

A. Parents have been conditioned to say no. They do it without thinking. And you are the reason why. Think back to your baby years. With all the counter space in the kitchen, why did you always try to put your hand on top of the stove? When you were playing outside in beautiful grass, what made the street more attractive? What about the time you found your dad's screwdriver? What did you do with it? Stick it in your eye, in an electrical socket, or in the toilet? You did everything with it but tighten screws. As you grew older it got worse—like knocking the car out of gear and sailing down the driveway at the ripe old age of four!

To ensure your very survival, your parents have learned to instantly and automatically say, "No!"

To get them to say yes, save your requests for the kinds of things your parents are most likely to let you do. Second, if possible, bring the subject up several days before you need to know. This gives them time to think and gives you more time to negotiate (not to be confused with aggravate). Third, when you do bring it up, present it in such a way as to show your parents you've really thought it through. For example, if you wanted to go on a trip with the youth group over the weekend, but a major paper was due on Monday, tell them you will have your paper finished by Thursday night. Fourth, realize everything depends on timing. Ask your folks when they are most likely to hear what you're saying, not just before bedtime or right after a day's work. The best time may be right after a peaceful dinner. Finally, if they say no, try your best to respond positively. Don't keep bugging them. Just smile and tell them thanks for thinking about it. They will probably wonder what's gotten in to you. But it's amazing how far a great attitude will go in changing your parent's mind. It may take a few more "no's," but your new attitude will work wonders on them.

Q. Is it right that I'm forced to go to church each week? Doesn't the constitution guarantee me freedom of religion?

A. Look at it this way. If you do go to church, it's not going to hurt you. It might even help you. But if you don't go to church, your parents will probably kill you. Considering the consequences, going to church seems a whole lot better choice.

As long as you live under their roof, and they are responsible for taking care of you, you need to do what they ask.

Q. My parents are always getting on me about rock music. Why should they care what I listen to?

A. Some parents don't want their kids listening to rock music, but not always for the same reason. One of the reasons has to do with the volume level of your music. Even you have to admit that when your house can be seen shaking from across the street, the music is a little too loud. And it makes matters worse when your parents disagree with the style of your music. Put yourself in their shoes. Imagine having to involuntarily listen to funeral music at maximum volume. You would do a little complaining yourself.

Your parents may also be concerned about your hearing. We said your parents may also be concerned about your hearing. Listening at the level of volume you normally do for prolonged periods of time can damage your hearing.

They may also be concerned about how you use your time. A lot of students go to an extreme and waste a great deal of time listening to rock when they could be doing homework, cleaning their rooms, or hundreds of similarly delightful tasks.

Q. *Is rock music wrong?*

A. Many people say it is wrong because of the beat. That misses the point altogether. The Bible doesn't speak to the beat of the music any more than it speaks to how long Sunday school should last.

The Bible does speak about the messages we allow to enter our minds. Philippians 4:8 says, "Finally, brethren, whatever is true, whatever is honorable, whatever is right, whatever is pure, whatever is lovely, whatever is of good repute, if there is any excellence and if anything worthy of praise, let your mind dwell on these things."

Christian rock communicates that kind of message. But does secular rock? No way. You know as well as anyone the themes secular rock music presents. Even if you don't "listen to the lyrics," they will affect you. Romans 12:2 says, "And do not be conformed to this world, but be transformed by the renewing of your mind, that you may prove what the will of God is, that which is good and acceptable and perfect."

If you enjoy rock, get into some good Christian rock.

You'll love it and will probably be surprised at how much your thought life will improve.

Q. *I want some space but my parents keep hanging on. How can I get them to let go a bit and allow me to grow up?*

A. You are fighting the War of Independence. You want, and rightly so, to have more and more freedoms. You'd like to have your own car, stay out later, buy a big ticket item or make your own decisions. Your parents, on the other hand, aren't letting go of the reins quite as fast as you want them to. Here's why. First, no doubt about it, as a teenager, you are becoming an adult. Trouble is, however, sometimes you still act like a kid. When your parents think of turning the keys over to your sovereign control, the images of your being an adult don't always flash across their minds. Instead, they remember you as a a three-year-old crashing your tricycle into the only tree in the entire yard. What reinforces these pictures are the times when lately you have reverted from the fine, mature person you are into a whining, obnoxious kid again. Your parents must have their minds reprogrammed before they turn completely loose. And this will take some time.

A second reason, which will be harder to understand than the first, is that your parents love you and may not want you to grow up too fast. They enjoy having you around and dependent on them. They realize they only have a few short years left with you. To you that may seem like eternity. But to them the time flies by fast. They may try to slow the inevitable by not letting go.

Q. What can I do to get my parents to trust me?

A. Students often complain that their parents don't trust them with being out late, using the car, who they have as friends, spending their money, what they do on dates, making decisions, telling the truth, buying their clothes, completing their chores, or doing their homework. And the list goes on!

For your parents to trust you, you must demonstrate responsibility. That means you follow through on and finish what you've committed yourself to do. Every time you demonstrate that you are responsible, your parents' trust level grows.

The problem is that trust is like a savings account. It takes forever to build it up to a significant level. But you can delete it in just a fraction of a second. Each time you act responsibly you make a deposit. Each time you blow a responsibility you make a withdrawal. Withdrawals are easy. Deposits represent a lot of hard work.

If you want your parents' trust in you to grow, reduce your withdrawals. Talk to your parents about what ways, if any, you are losing their trust, then change. Second, follow through on your present responsibilities. Be especially concerned with even the "little responsibilities." Your parents probably think like this, "If I can't trust him to do something little like take the garbage out, how can I trust him to do something big like take someone's daughter out?"

Q. How can I get my parents to stop asking me so many questions?

A. Would you ask your boyfriend a lot of questions if you saw on TV that a trend had just been discovered of boyfriends breaking up with their girlfriends? Sure you would, because you would be afraid.

Parents fear too. Most of what they hear on TV, radio or read in the papers are of teenage drug problems, teenagers committing suicide, adolescent sexual activity on the rise, or of teenage crime running rampant.

Rarely do they hear any good news, not even something like "teenager lasts two weeks without getting one pimple!"

You want them to ask less questions? Then communicate. Your parents love you. They want to protect you. Talk to them about the juicy stuff: who likes whom, who broke up with whom, etc. They like to hear the latest gossip-of-the-day type stuff from you. It may also add a few years to their lives because they won't worry so much about you.

Q. My parents never believe me. Any suggestions?

A. To get your parents to believe you, you must first ask why they don't trust you. Generally, it is because they have discovered that you have lied about something in the past.

Lying has terrible consequences. If someone has lied to you, how do you know when they're lying or telling the truth?

To get your parents to believe you, ask them to forgive you for any and every time you have lied to them in the past. And don't stop with just asking forgiveness for the lies you've said with your mouth. Also ask forgiveness for the lies you've said with your actions—like having a bunch of friends over at the house when it was forbidden.

Second, learn to admit when you blow it. Nobody believes you always live a perfect life. So when they hear you volunteer the fact that you blew it, but now you are sorry for what you did, they will believe you much more quickly than if you never admit your shortcomings and failures.

Q. *My parents won't let me date a guy until I'm sixteen. They don't think I can handle myself if caught in a tempting situation. What can I do to convince them I'm trustworthy?*

A. It's not you they are worried about as much as it is the guy who wants to take you out. Understand that your parents have taken care of you now for years. They changed your diapers, fed you, clothed you, did everything for you. Now you want to go out on a date with some creep (from their perspective) who doesn't even ask them to double with the two of you!

Being old enough to date isn't determined by a magic number (like sixteen). It has a great deal to do with your spiritual maturity. But physical age does have a lot to do with it. (Check out those questions in the chapter on dating.) The older you get the longer you have to nail down your convictions as well as discover the maneuvers guys use. Be glad you have parents who care. And be grateful they have quit trying to clothe you, feed you and change your diapers.

Q. *Why is my dad always on my case about being lazy? All he ever does is nag, nag, nag.*

A. The issue is not laziness. Anyone who can go to school for seven hours, go to band practice, watch four and one half hours of TV, talk on the telephone to three different guys and four different girlfriends for a total of three and one half hours, as well as do two hours of homework in less than five minutes is definitely not lazy.

The issue is priorities. You and your dad have a difference in perspective on what is a priority and what isn't. For example, you see watching TV, talking on the telephone and going out with your friends as a priority. On the other hand, your dad sees things like washing the car, cutting the grass and cleaning your room as much more important.

To calm your dad down you need to see what's most important in his opinion. When you do what he wants done, when he wants it done, he won't nag you as much. You will have also taken major steps toward bringing peace to earth and goodwill to all men.

Q. Why must my parents embarrass me in front of my friends?

A. It doesn't take much for a parent to ruin things, does it? Like hanging around pretending they are tidying up when your friends are over, but it's obvious they are trying to listen in on the conversation. Or trying to be "cool" by talking about the latest music groups and the only group they mention is Lawrence Welk. Or how about when they kiss you in public?

Definitely try to communicate your feelings to them. But be sensitive. Rumor has it there are some things you do that embarrasses them. Perhaps you could work out an arrangement that would be mutually beneficial, causing nobody ever to be embarrassed again.

Q. *Why don't my parents love me?*

A. You must get it through your head that your parents really don't wake up every morning wondering, "How can I increase my child's suffering today?" Your parents do love you. But they don't always show it in the ways you would like them to.

Actually, when it comes to love, your mom and dad have a big S stamped across their chests. And it doesn't stand for super, and definitely not for stupid. It stands for the ways your parents show their love, by their Service and by their Sacrifice.

Serving someone demonstrates an even greater depth of their love. Think about this: How many plates, glasses, forks, knives, spoons, pots and pans does your mom wash for you each day? Multiply that by 365. What does that total each year? _____

And don't forget all the tasks your dad did to the car or around the house to make life more comfortable for you and your family. Think of the number of days your parents work to provide for you. How many of those mornings do you think they would rather stay home and relax? _____

You may argue that your mom and dad have to cook meals or wash clothes anyway—it can't be that much trouble to wash a few more plates or fold a few more clothes. That may be true, but consider how much they sacrifice for you.

Who stayed up all night with you when you were sick? Who works extra hours to pay for all the things you want? (adapted from *Parents: Raising Them Properly* pp. 53–54).

So the next time you doubt their love, look at the ways they do know how to express it, not just the ways they don't.

Q. I feel like my parents don't love me because I can never measure up to their expectations. What does it take to satisfy them?

A. Parents have a funny way of talking sometimes. You bring home five A's and one B and what do they say, not, "Great! Five A's and only one B," but "Why didn't you make straight A's?!"

You come home late because you've been in an accident. Do they ask, "Are you okay?" No. Instead they ask, "What were you doing over on that side of town anyway?"

Jesus' parents did the same thing to Him. Read Luke 2:41–51 if you don't believe it. Every parent speaks that way. Sometimes it comes from a desire that their child become the best, do the best (like straight A's) and have the best. Other times it comes from just plain fear.

Take the "What were you doing on that side of town anyway?" as an example. Their logic goes like this. "I love you. And it scared me when I found out you were in a wreck. If you had not driven over there you might not have had an accident."

Remember your parents talk that way because they do love you, in spite of what it feels like.

Q. Are parents always right? Why can't they ever admit that they are wrong?

A. Parents aren't always right. Nobody's perfect. But parents probably aren't wrong as often as you think. They are just approaching the situation from an entirely different perspective.

But you're right. When they are wrong, it is hard for most of them to admit it. They tend to think if they admit they are wrong you will no longer respect their authority and they will lose control of you.

So make it easier on them. The next time you catch them in obvious error (you know, like the times you can document your answer from three different sources), don't rub it in. If they eventually say, "I was wrong," then tell them something like, "That's okay, I thought I was wrong once, but I found out later that I was mistaken."

Q. *Is it wrong to argue with your parents when you know you are right and they are wrong?*

A. If your attitude is wrong, it is wrong to argue anytime, even if you're right. Ephesians 6:2 says, "Honor your father and mother (which is the first commandment with a promise)." If you have committed your life to the Lordship of Christ, you have no other option. You must show honor at all times.

When you find yourself in those situations, you might go away and let things cool down a bit. No, let them cool down a lot. If you feel that it would be beneficial for your parents to know the answer (not just know you were right), you might carefully bring it up again. If you don't think it would benefit them or if they begin to get upset, then drop it immediately.

Q. What can I do? My parents and I fight all the time.

A. Your family can be different. Since it takes two to fight, you can make a few changes that will bring much peace to your family.

Often some comment from your parents may set you off and the fight begins. Some of those might include:

> "As long as you're living under my roof . . . ."
> "Because I said so, that's why . . . ."
> "How many times have I told you?"
> "Who was on the phone?"
> "Money doesn't grow on trees."
> "What did you learn today?"
> "Good things don't come easy."
> "Get a job!"
> "Don't wait till the last minute."
> "Who's going to be at the party?"
> "Go read a book."
> "You're the oldest. You should be more responsible."
> "Go ask your father."
> "You're old enough to know better."
> "I love you, *but* . . . ."
> "Turn down that stereo!"

Identify which ones tick you off. Then decide ahead of time how you will respond.

All too often we respond defensively. You may recognize some of these weapons:

1. *Complaining.* "All the other kids get to do it." "I always have to stay home."

2. *Criticism.* "You're behind the times!" "You're not fair!"
3. *Anger.* Slam doors. Yell, shout, scream.
4. *Silence.* Sigh. Roll eyes.
5. *Running out.* Run to your room. Run to a friend's.

(adapted from:
Parents: Raising Them Properly p. 27)

To end the conflict in your home, it is a must that you learn how to respond as Christ would have you do. He wants you to respond with a positive attitude. If you blow it, ask them to forgive you and start all over.

Q. *How can I keep from killing my brothers and sisters?*

A. You're definitely not the first to think about this. Conflict between siblings has been around from the beginning. Take the first two brothers on the face of the earth, Cain and Abel (two of Adam and Eve's kids). Cain became so angry he actually did kill his brother. King David's kids did not get along any better. Jacob's boys had a creative twist. They just dropped kid brother Joseph in a deep hole and left him. Later they sold him into slavery and made a few bucks off the kid.

This is not to say that you should copy these Bible people and then tell your parents you were only trying to live your life according to the Bible.

Granted, it does irritate even the most mature teenager to come home and find someone has trespassed on his property (his room) or used his stuff (albums or clothes) or to have a brother or sister constantly spying on him (especially when he's entertaining a date).

So what should you do? Don't get mad, get even!

Here are a few simple suggestions from the Bible on how God wants you to get even with your brothers and sisters. Luke 6:27–31 says, "But I say to you who hear, love your enemies, do good to those who hate you, bless those who curse you, pray for those who mistreat you. Whoever hits you on the cheek, offer him the other also; and whoever takes away your coat, do not withhold your shirt from him either. Give to everyone who asks of you, and whoever takes away what is yours, do not demand it back. And just as you want people to treat you, treat them in the same way."

If your brother or sister hates you, insults you, hits you, wears some of your clothes without asking, or wants to borrow your most prized possessions, these verses tell you how to respond.

It doesn't seem as much fun compared to what you used to do, does it? What could give more pleasure than tying your little brother to a tree outside and throwing rocks at him, or flushing your sister's head in the toilet? No, it's not as much fun at first. But as time passes you'll discover your home life is a whole lot happier.

Q.   What should I do if my parent is an alcoholic? It's so hard to live with them.

A.   Sometimes parents have significant problems themselves. One of the ways they try to cope is through alcohol. When they drink, their behavior can change, often becoming argumentative and violent, sometimes even abusive.

There are no easy answers. But if you live with an alcoholic parent, try to take your focus off of their problems and think about what needs they might have. Often, it is a spiritual need that only Jesus Christ can meet. So pray. Ask Christ to meet your mom's or dad's deepest needs and to give you a supernatural love for them.

If you live in an abusive situation, it would be wise to seek counsel from your youth minister or pastor about what to do.

Q. *Why do mom and dad talk about getting a divorce?*

A. There are times when mom and dad may have problems getting along. One thing or another may cause this. The major stress points in a marriage are not kids as much as financial problems, lack of communication and lack of trust.

When parents, or anyone for that matter, get under pressure, their sensitivity level goes up. As a result they get easily offended by their spouse and begin to fight.

One of the deadliest weapons in their arsenal is divorce. They know that by merely bringing the subject up that they can inflict great pain.

During times when they talk like that, you too must fight but not the same fight that your parents are having. Your fight is in the spiritual realm. When you discover that they are or have been talking about divorce, go into your room and assume the role of a prayer warrior. Ephesians 6:10–12, 18 says, "Finally, be strong in the Lord, and in the strength of His might. Put on the full armor of God, that you may be able to stand firm against the schemes of the devil. For our struggle is not against flesh and blood, but against the rulers, against the powers, against the world forces of this darkness, against the spiritual forces of wickedness in the heavenly places. . . . With all prayer and petition pray at all times in the Spirit,

and with this in view, be on the alert with all persever-
ance and petition for all the saints."

Q. *My parents recently got a divorce. I feel like my life is
ruined. What can I do?*

A. Unfortunately, divorce has become quite common-
place. Half your friends have already experienced, or
will experience, divorce if the current divorce levels
persist. Divorce can never be pleasant or positive. A
divorce often leaves family members feeling angry, bitter, sad, confused and betrayed—just to mention a few
reactions.

One of the things a divorce damages the most is your
self-image. Your thinking might go like this, "If my parents don't love me enough to stay together, I must not be
very valuable or important to them. If I'm not important
or valuable to my parents who are supposed to love me,
then I'll never be loved by anyone again."

With your self-image shattered you can find yourself
becoming more and more apathetic. Your grades may suffer, your friendships may take a nose dive, you may even
run from God for a while.

Understand this—*your life isn't ruined!* You are special. You are valuable. You are important.

Just because your parents have gone through a divorce doesn't mean you can't have a productive and significant life. Avoid letting your anger and bitterness turn
you away from all that is positive and good in life. Resist
the tendency to give up and waste your life.

Find a wise Christian friend, like your youth pastor
or Sunday school teacher. Talk your feelings through
with them.

Q. Why do I feel like it's my fault that my parents got a divorce?

A. You probably feel like it's your fault because you remember all the fighting and arguing that took place toward the end. You wonder if things would have been different if you had only given in a little more. Catch this: It is not your fault that your parents got a divorce. They are the ones who made the decision, not you. Whenever you have those guilty feelings, do two things. Remember it wasn't because of you that they got a divorce. And secondly, instead of thinking about whose fault it was, use your energy to pray that God would work in a significant way in the lives of both your parents.

Q. How can I get along with my stepparent?

A. It is often hard, especially at first, to get along with a stepmom or stepdad. Deep down there may be resentment. This person has taken the place of your real mom or dad. You wished for months that your real parents would remarry but now that will never happen. Often your "new" parent will ask you to do things your "real" one never asked you, like make up your bed. So now, not only did your dad trade in your mom for a different model, but it seems to you like he made a terrible trade.

What makes things worse is the favoritism a stepparent may show his or her own kids. They never get in trouble because they can do no wrong. So you go to school and join the "I hate my stepparent club."

If you want to get along with a stepparent, you must learn to accept and receive this new person. No, they will not take the place you have in your heart for your real parent. But you aren't being disloyal to your real parent by finding at least a corner in your heart for your stepparent. It may take time before you ever feel differently about them, but if you don't begin to reach out, you will never feel differently.

Begin today. Think of something you two can do together. When you are alone, tell your new parent how hard it has been to accept him or her. Assure him or her that even though your esteem for them may be small now, by God's grace, it will grow bigger as time goes on.

Q. Can you help? My parents are divorced. I'm being pulled between my real mom and my real dad. If it doesn't stop soon, I feel like I'll be split right down the middle.

A. This is a tough situation to be in. Your dad makes you feel guilty for spending time with your mom, so you spend more time with your dad only to find out your mom now feels left out. And it's not only your time they want. Each wants to be assured that you love them best.

To survive in that situation, keep clearly in focus why they act that way. They both have deep needs to be loved. Take every effort to assure them, but don't get caught in the "Who do you love the most?" trap. Tell them you love them both the same.

When it comes to putting pressure on you to spend more time, realize you won't be able to satisfy them regardless of how much time you spend with them. You aren't the answer to their needs. Spend the time you can but don't feel guilty about the time you can't.

Q. *Can God put my family back together?*

A. It's possible, but it doesn't always happen. You may have to live the rest of your life with all the realities a divorce brings: new school, new financial situation (probably a lot less money than before), a new house, maybe even a new family.

But don't let the discouragement get you down. God can put *you* back together. Right now you probably feel like the divorce broke your life into a million pieces. If so, God can put you back together into an even better person than you were before. For God to do that you must respond the way He wants you to.

Some of the wrong ways to deal with the divorce include:

I'll withdraw. Everyone is laughing at me, my family is a failure, and I'll be better off if I just keep my mouth shut.

I'll fight. I dare anyone to laugh at me. No one cares about me, that's for sure. So I'm going to look out for myself and no one had better get in my way!

I'll be a clown. If I act happy and joke around all the time, no one will guess that my parents divorced.

I'll deny reality. I'll tell my friends that my dad is just away on business. I will never have friends over, and I'll talk about my dad like he is the greatest in the world even though I'll only see him once or twice a year.

I'll conform. Whatever the crowd does, I'll do it too, and no one will know how different I feel because of the divorce.

I'll compensate. I've been hurt, but I won't go down. I'll be the very best at what I can do and everyone will be so busy congratulating me on my success they won't notice that my family has fallen to pieces.

(adapted from: *Mom and Dad Don't Live Together Anymore* by Gary and Angela Hunt, San Bernardino: Here's Life, p. 19).

In God's strength, respond positively by learning from the experience and move on with life. Romans 8:28–29 says, "And we know that God causes all things to work together for good to those who love God, to those who are called according to His purpose. For whom He foreknew, He also predestined to become conformed to the image of His Son, that He might be the first-born among many brethren."

God desires to use every situation in your life to conform you to the image of His Son Jesus Christ. Don't run from your past, run to God. Allow Him to use your past to make you into the person He wants you to become. In the end, you will be a much stronger person because of what you've been through.

Q. Why is my dad so old-fashioned?

A. At the risk of turning you off, an old cliché can best answer that. It is a phase you're passing through. Don't believe that? Well, try to look at the big picture. At the following stages in life you think:

At age 4: My Daddy can do anything!
At age 6: My Dad knows a lot! A whole lot!
At age 8: My father doesn't know about some things.
At age 12: Of course, my father doesn't know.

At age 14: My father is so old-fashioned that he's hopeless.

At age 20: My old man is in another time zone.

At age 25: My Dad might know something about that.

At age 35: Maybe we should get Dad's advice on it.

At age 60: Wonder what Dad would have thought about it?

At age 70: I wish that I could discuss it with Dad again.

How many of these have described your thoughts about your dad so far? Probably quite a few.

So be patient. Give yourself some time. In a few more years your dad will grow out of it.

Q. *How can I get my non-Christian dad to become a Christian?*

A. You can choose from several approaches. Let's begin with the least effective and move to the most effective.

One approach is the "Flame-thrower Finale" (Please note. It is called the finale because you usually only get one chance at this per lifetime). You sneak up on your dad while he's reading in his most comfortable chair. Then you carefully light the bottom of his paper, making sure you don't burn yourself. Then (timing is everything here), as soon as he yells and throws the paper into the air, you jump on the chair, one foot firmly planted on each armrest. As you look down on your white-faced father, announce in your most authoritative voice, "You are just a heartbeat away from hell. At any moment you could die and the next moment you would experience for the rest of eternity, the fires of hell. Dad, you must turn or burn."

Another approach is called the "Condemnation Confrontation." You wait for your dad to come home from a really hard day at work. Then you meet him eyeball to eyeball and begin a complete and thorough rendition of what a totally depraved sinner he is. Be sure to point out how spiritual and righteous Jesus has made you. Give him no chance to talk or ask questions. Just keep blasting away with both barrels.

The third approach is called the "Balanced Attack." It's made up of the perfect mixture of prayer, example of godliness at home and sensitive sharing of what Jesus Christ has done in your life. Most students have found this approach the most effective.

Q. My parents say I don't respect them. I do everything they ask me to do. What's the big deal?

A. How would your friends feel if you treated them like you do your mother? You wouldn't have many friends, would you?

Actions aren't enough if the attitude isn't right. God, as well as your parents, wants you to have both. Ephesians 6:1, 2 says, "Children, obey your parents in the Lord, for this is right. Honor your father and mother (which is the first commandment, with a promise)." Obedience has to do with actions. Honor has to do with attitude. You need both.

Q. *How can I show my parents that I respect them?*

A. The Book of Proverbs describes four different ways. You can honor them in:

- *speaking:* Proverbs 20:20 says, "He who curses his father or his mother, His lamp will go out in time of darkness."
- *listening:* Proverbs 5:7 says, "Now then, my sons, listen to me, and do not depart from the words of my mouth."
- *looking:* Proverbs 30:17 says, "The eye that mocks a father, and scorns a mother, the ravens of the valley will pick it out, and the young eagles will eat it."
- *acting:* Proverbs 6:20, 21 says, "My son, observe the commandment of your father, and do not forsake the teaching of your mother; bind them continually on your heart; tie them around your neck."

Translated: When you talk to them, avoid whining, complaining and yelling. When you listen to them, really listen. Don't let your mind wander regardless how long "The Speech" goes on. And when they tell you to do something, do it even if they aren't around or if nobody's watching.

Q. *How can I show my parents I really love them?*

A. Great question. Here are some suggestions to get you started:

1. Say "I love you."
2. Invite your parents to school activities.

3. Visit Dad or Mom at work.
4. Bring Mom flowers.
5. Wash the car without being asked.

Showing your parents you love them might not be easy. But one day when they are gone, you will have some fantastic guilt-free memories.

2 | Self-Image

Q. *Every time I look in the mirror I think, "God really blew it when He put me together." Is it possible for God to make a mistake on one of His creations?*

A. All of us at one time or another have looked in the mirror and gagged over what we saw. Perhaps, gals, you were disgusted with your hippo-hips. Or, guys, you realized why you had to run around the shower to get wet— you were so skinny the shower spray would miss you otherwise. The worst experience is getting ready to leave for a date and taking that one last look in the mirror. Then you realize a new purple pimple has just popped out, right on the end of your nose.

You yell, "Thanks a lot, God. You'll never know how much I appreciate being Mister or Miss Zit City. Why me, God? Why did you have to blow it on me? Wouldn't my little brother have been a much better victim if you had to make a mistake?"

Listen carefully. You are not alone. All of us have felt that way, even your school's homecoming queen and student body president. But the truth of the matter is that God doesn't make mistakes. He didn't make a mistake on you or anyone else. Whether you feel like you are too tall, too short, too big, too little, or even too ugly, God made you just as you are because He thinks you are perfect.

Having a hard time believing that? Then check out Psalm 139:13–18.

Q. My nose looks like Miss Piggy's. Why was I made this way?

A. God loves variety. That's why no two flowers are the same, no two snowflakes are the same and no two people are the same. He didn't want you to be "just like everybody else" because you are special to Him. He made you different because you deserve to be different.

Differences are what make people interesting and unique. Besides, how much fun would it be if we all looked alike? It wouldn't. If we were all the same, no one would be special. But since we are all different, we are all special.

Q. Why don't I like the way I look?

A. The media has played a major role in this. It communicates that a good-looking person has to look a certain way. Guys have to be tall, dark and handsome. Women have to be proportioned just right. A good-looking person will never have a bad complexion. They will only wear certain clothes, and those clothes will be worn a certain way.

So the media has created its own standard of what it considers a good-looking person. Perhaps you have accepted that standard as the ultimate standard. If you don't look like that then you probably don't like the way you look.

Q. Should I try to look the way the media says a person should look?

A. It's okay (in most cases) to try to look like the person the media seeks to sell. Take fashions, for example. Even

Adam and Eve changed to animal skins when fig leaves went out of style. So if you are still into bellbottom pants, polyester suits or bouffant hairdos, it's okay to change.

But if you are going to try physically to look like the media's image of the perfect body, look out. You are in for some frustration. Why? Two reasons. First, the media's standard is constantly changing. In the '60s, Twiggy was the standard. (If you don't remember her, she looked like a toothpick with blonde hair.) In the '80s it was Joan Collins. In the '90s Diane Brill has been chosen as "The Shape of the '90s." The choice of Brill according to *Newsweek* Magazine, "proves the bust is back and the bigger, the better." Now what are the Twiggys of the '90s going to do? If they don't look at themselves the way God sees them, they will be as frustrated as the Brills of the '60s were.

The second reason is this: You are constantly changing. Let's take you guys for example. Today you may look like the Tom Cruises (a standard for the '80s). But a few years from now you will probably be bald and overweight like your father. That's just the way it works. If you base your self-worth on the way you look, you are going to be frustrated.

Your self-worth must be based on a different value system than that of the media.

Q. I want to look different. What can I do?

A. There's a lot you can do. Take those flabby thighs, for example. Medical advances now offer "suction lipectomy." This procedure involves a small incision at the top of the leg where a suction tube is inserted to suck out all the fat cells. The procedure is safe and permanent because the fat cells are gone! And it might only cost you a few thousand dollars.

More and more people are surrendering their faces and bodies to modern medicine, hoping to look prettier, younger, thinner or more assertive. Consider your options:

Procedure	Fee
Hair transplants	$ 300–$ 500
Mentoplasty (Chin implants)	$ 250–$3000
Abdominoplasty (Tummy tuck)	$1500–$5000
Suction Lipectomy (Fat removal)	$ 300–$4000
Rhytidectomy (face-lift)	$1500–$8000
Rhinoplasty (nose)	$1000–$4500
Blepharoplasty (Eye tucks)	$ 600–$4000
Breast augmentation	$1000–$3000

We are not suggesting you try these. But you need to see the extent some people will go as well as the legitimate opportunities available. Later steps will be given that you can take to help you look your best. But instead of answering your question with an answer, let us answer it with a question. Why do you want to look different? Is it possible you are struggling with a poor self-image?

Q. What do you mean by self-image?

A. Your self-image is the mental picture you have of yourself. It started to be formed the moment you were born. By the age of five or six your self-concept, the person you think you are in relationship to others, is so firmly established that you will resist efforts to change it.

This does not mean you can't change it. Many people have moved from a negative to a positive self-image and from a positive to a negative self-image. It's just that once you get an idea of who you think you are, you don't change very easily. And since your self-image affects every responsibility and relationship that you have, it is very important to acquire a healthy self-image as early in life as you possibly can.

Q. What's the difference between a negative, positive and healthy self-image?

A. If you have a negative self-image then you don't think very well of yourself. People with negative self-images are often pessimistic, lacking in confidence, extremely sensitive to the opinion of others, self-conscious about their appearance or performance, constantly wondering what people think of them, carrying a chip on their shoulders, clinging in relationships, unable to receive another's love, looking for possessions to make them happy, talking negatively about themselves or others. They are worry warts, perfectionists, legalistic, overly sensitive and compare themselves to others (adapted from *His Image . . . My Image*, p. 43).

On the other hand, if you have a positive self-image, you think highly of yourself. But this doesn't mean you have a healthy self-image. A healthy image is seeing yourself as God sees you.

If you have a healthy self-image you will think highly of yourself because God thinks highly of you. But not all people with positive self-images have a healthy self-image. Some people think they are the greatest because of the way they look or their intelligence or some ability they have that is outstanding. But a simple car accident could change all three of those in a moment's time.

In contrast, when you see who you are in Jesus Christ, nothing or no one can ever change that. You will have both a healthy and positive view of yourself.

Q. Why is it important to have a healthy self-image?

A. Research has shown that people act in harmony with the mental picture they have of themselves. If they see themselves as failures, they will act like failures. So your self-image affects every relationship you will ever have. For example, if you think you're the worst person on the face of the earth, then here's what will tend to happen in your relationship with your:

- *friendships*—no one likes being around you because you are constantly cutting yourself down.
- *parents*—not very close, because you feel that they don't love you.
- *dating*—you're afraid to go out with anyone.
- *God*—you find it hard to believe He wants the best for you.

But what if you think you're the greatest person in the world?

- *friendships*—your conceit drives people away.
- *parents*—you become "Mr. or Miss Know-It-All."
- *dating*—you focus only on yourself.
- *God*—you feel like you don't need Him.

A healthy self-image enables you to meet not only your own personal needs but also the needs of others.

You can be the kind of friend, son or daughter, date and Christian that God has called you to be.

Q. *Is the concept of self-image biblical?*

A. Yes! Check out these verses:

> "For through the grace given to me I say to every man among you not to think more highly of himself than he ought to think; but to think so as to have sound judgment, as God has allotted to each a measure of faith" (Romans 12:3).
>
> "Do nothing from selfishness or empty conceit, but with humility of mind let each of you regard one another as more important than himself; do not merely look out for your own personal interests, but also for the interests of others" (Philippians 2:3, 4).
>
> "And have put on the new self who is being renewed to a true knowledge according to the image of the One who created him" (Colossians 3:10).

God wants you to see yourself the same way He sees you, no more and no less.

Q. *What factors contributed to my self-image?*

A. The initial development of your self-image lies in your relationships with your parents. You learned who you were and what you were like from them.

Your parents' evaluations of you were transferred to your young mind. You saw yourself in light of their thoughts and actions toward you. From their attitudes you sensed their feelings about you. Those experiences, even if long ago forgotten, served to form your self-concepts.

Thus the everyday experiences of your childhood (not solely the traumatic ones) were what shaped your self-image. The general atmosphere in your families contributed more to your view of yourselves than any single event (adapted from *His Image . . . My Image*, p. 58).

A second influence in forming your self-image is your appearance. Think about it. Who gets most of the attention at school? Those who have "good looks," right? That's why people spend so much time and money on how they look, because appearance can get one the attention he so desires. So if you have acne, big ears, bad teeth, no chest, skinny arms, a fat stomach, knocked knees and pigeoned toes you may tend to grow up feeling one way about yourself than if you have beautiful hair, great teeth and a perfect figure.

Another influence that probably affected your self-image in a significant way is your intelligence level. Whether you were called a dummy or a whiz kid, growing up can have a definite impact on how you see yourself.

Your abilities contribute a great deal as well to your self-image. Being a great piano player or athlete could have compensated for feeling that you were ugly.

Significant experiences from the past also affect how your self-image developed. Suppose you rescued a small child from drowning and you were recognized on the front page of the paper. Or you won a million dollars in some contest and were featured on all the major TV talk shows. Or imagine if you split your pants in front of the entire student body. These kinds of experiences play a major role in how you view yourself.

Because few people have perfect parents, great looks, superior intelligence, outstanding abilities and positive experiences throughout their lives, most struggle with low views of themselves.

Q. *My parents have always told me that I would never amount to anything. Why has this affected me so much?*

A. Your self-image is composed of conclusions you have reached about yourself. These conclusions follow this sequence:

Stages	Example
You hear it.	"You're stupid."
You think about it.	Am I stupid?
An experience reinforces it.	You make a big mistake and your friends laugh at you.
You feel it.	I feel so stupid.
You believe it.	I am told I'm stupid, I act that way, I feel that way. It must be true. I am stupid.

That's why it's so important to know what God says about you. As you read the Bible you learn what God thinks of you. And what God thinks of you is what is true about you.

Q. *Why do people always want me to be like somebody else? Should I try to be like somebody I'm not?*

A. Yes and no.

God has made you uniquely different from everybody else. And He wants you to stay different. God wants you to realize that trying to be as pretty as a homecoming queen, as smart as the valedictorian or as gifted as the school jock will only lead to frustration. He wants you to accept yourself as the person He's created you to be.

On the other hand, there is somebody you should strive to be like. Someone even God wants you to copy. And that's His Son, Jesus Christ. Romans 8:29 says, "For whom He foreknew, He also predestined to become conformed to the image of His Son, that He might be the first-born among many brethren."

Q. How in the world can I be like Jesus Christ? I can't even swim, much less walk on water.

A. God wants you to be like His Son in your character, that is, what you are like on the inside. There is no outward ideal when it comes to looks or abilities. But there is an inward ideal. It's found in Galatians 5:22, 23, "But the fruit of the Spirit is love, joy, peace, patience, kindness, goodness, faithfulness, gentleness, self-control; against such things there is no law."

God wants you to allow His Spirit to control you so you will be like His Son.

Q. Why am I always comparing myself to everybody else?

A. You compare yourself because you want to know how well you measure up. If you are doing well you can feel good about yourself. If you aren't as pretty, smart, rich or gifted as the other person, then you can't feel good about yourself.

The trouble with comparison comes from comparing yourself to the wrong measure—other people. Because every person is different, you will always find someone you think is better or worse than you are. This will leave you filled with frustration or pride.

God doesn't want you to compare yourself based on

an outward measure, but on an inward measure. Instead of asking, "Am I as good as so-n-so?" ask, "Do I have the character of Christ that God wants me to have?" That will keep your focus where it needs to be.

Q. Why do I feel so inadequate?

A. All too often we judge ourselves by the world's standard and discover we don't measure up. We seem foolish and weak compared to those around us. First Corinthians 1:27 says, "But God has chosen the foolish things of the world to shame the wise, and God has chosen the weak things of the world to shame the things which are strong." This means that God can use your foolishness (lack of brilliance, lack of popularity, lack of experience) and your weaknesses (lack of strength, lack of looks, lack of abilities) to shame the world's system. How? By demonstrating His power through you. God's power makes you adequate for every responsibility He has called you to fulfill. Second Corinthians 3:5 says, "Not that we are adequate in ourselves to consider anything as coming from ourselves, but our adequacy is from God."

Q. I feel like a worm. Why do I feel so worthless?

A. Feeling worthless is a sign of a poor self-image. You feel worthless because you don't realize how valuable you are.

A Yale scientist has said that every dry pound of you is worth about $112,247. Because about 68 percent of your body is water, you can calculate your dry weight by multiplying your full weight by 0.32. Then figure your total value by multiplying that dry weight by $112,247. If you weigh 125, for instance, you possess 40 pounds of dry weight that means your body is worth about four and a half million dollars!

You may argue that worth or value is determined by what is paid for it. So it doesn't matter if you are worth 4½ million if no one is willing to pay the price. That's true. But a price far more valuable than dollars has already been paid for you—the precious blood of Jesus Christ the Lord. He died on the cross to bring you to God. Do you want to know how much you are worth? Then figure up how much the life of Christ was worth. First Peter 1:18, 19 will give you a hint:

"Knowing that you were not redeemed with perishable things like silver or gold from your futile way of life inherited from your forefathers, but with precious blood, as of a lamb unblemished and spotless, the blood of Christ."

Are you worthless? No! You are exceedingly valuable. Try to comprehend that. When you do, it will revolutionize your life!

Q. Why do I feel so insecure?

A. Most everyone can relate to that feeling. You have just gotten your hair styled differently and it was a complete flop. You wanted it a little bleached out but instead it's fluorescent orange. As you walk down the hallway you are convinced everyone is staring at you, then whispering to one another and laughing. You definitely don't feel confidence oozing out of your being.

We feel insecure when we don't know if we are going to be accepted or not. We look at ourselves with all of our shortcomings and wonder why anyone would ever want to spend time with us.

But you don't have to feel that way. You are accepted by the One who matters most—Jesus Christ. He accepts you just like you are, fluorescent orange hair and all. Hebrews 13:5 says, ". . . for He Himself has said 'I will never desert you, nor will I ever forsake you.'"

Now understand what we mean by this. If Jesus Christ, the Creator of the universe, accepts you, what does it matter if nobody else accepts you? That's not to say that you don't need people. You do. It's just that you don't need their acceptance to be a whole person. If that were the case, Jesus Himself and most of the disciples would never have been whole people. When you realize in your heart that Christ accepts you unconditionally, you are freed to remove your focus from yourself and put it on others. Most all of your friends feel insecure whether they act that way or not. They need someone who will help meet their needs by reaching out to them and pointing them to Jesus. Knowing the acceptance of Christ frees you from insecurity and releases you to be a confident friend.

Q. *Why am I so shy?*

A. When people don't accept themselves, their greatest fear is that their friends will reject them. Some people have the attitude that if they don't try to get their friends' acceptance they will be rejected. So these students become very outgoing, often to an extreme. You know, they are the guys who will do anything for attention, like eating the fish out of the aquarium in biology class.

Some other people have a different attitude. They think if they do try to get their friends' acceptance, they will be rejected. Their fear then keeps them in a little prison, refusing to let them out to experience life to its fullest.

Remember, it's not the end of the world if your friends reject you because Christ accepts you. Realize the significance of that truth and you'll break out of your prison. Your friends at school need what you have to offer.

Q. I won't do anything. I'm too afraid of blowing it. Why am I so afraid of failure?

A. You may have heard about PDA (public displays of affection), but have you ever heard of PBA (performance-based acceptance)? The world has ripped us off by selling us a lie. We have come to believe that our worth is based on what we do, not who we are.

It often starts at home. You know the feelings you experience when you show your parents your grades, and instead of bragging about the five A's, they begin nagging about the one B. Or the comments like, "Why can't you be like your older sister? She never. . . . " You go away thinking that to be accepted, you have to perform.

The great thing about being a Christian is you don't have to perform to be accepted. Christ has already performed perfectly for you. He came to earth and lived a perfect life for 33 years. When you became a Christian, His life became your life. Jesus took your failures and gave you His righteousness. Second Corinthians 5:21 says, "He made Him who knew no sin to be sin on our behalf, that we might become the righteousness of God in Him." When God looks at you now He sees perfection.

It's okay to fail. God won't reject you. He accepts you unconditionally. Step out in faith and seek to reach your full potential. You will never know what you are capable of accomplishing until you try.

Q. Why do I always want credit for everything that I do? I'm frustrated if I don't get recognized for the things I do.

A. You may want credit because you have bought in to the PBA lie (see above question). Your thinking may go like this: *If I do something good, people will notice. If people notice, I'll get credit. If I get credit, people will like me and think I'm special. I need for people to like me and think I'm special because I don't feel significant.*

When you become too concerned about what people think of your accomplishments, you have put your focus in the wrong place. You must put it back on God and what He thinks of you. He loves and accepts you just as you are.

So keep working hard, try to excel at the things you do. But do it for Christ's glory and not your own. Colossians 3:23, 24 says, "Whatever you do, do your work heartily, as for the Lord rather than for men; knowing that from the Lord you will receive the reward of the inheritance. It is the Lord Christ whom you serve."

Q. I don't have a problem thinking I'm worthless. If anything, I go to the other extreme. Is that wrong?

A. Not as long as you keep it in proper focus. Realize God gave you your abilities, talents, personality, looks and intelligence. And He gave them to you for a reason, to serve others. All too often students who have a lot going for them from the world's perspective forget the source of their gifts and become proud. People with a healthy self-image see themselves as God sees them, no more and no less. This leads to an attitude of humility, not pride. Philippians 2:3, 4 says "Do nothing from selfishness or empty conceit, but with humility of mind let each of you regard one another as more important than yourself; do not merely look out for your own personal interests, but also for the interests of others."

So don't feel badly that you have a positive self-image. God wants you to think highly of yourself because He thinks highly of you. But don't allow it to turn into pride either.

Q.   I often struggle with doubts about my salvation. Is that normal?

A.   Occasional thoughts about whether or not you are a Christian are common. But to struggle constantly about your salvation is definitely not normal. There are several reasons why you may be struggling. First, you may not be a Christian. Many people have joined a church thinking they were coming to Christ only to discover later that they never really invited Christ into their hearts. Another reason for struggling with your salvation may be that you have allowed unconfessed sin to accumulate in your life. But a common reason for doubting your salvation may be a poor self-image.

Here's how it works. You grow up thinking your parents don't love you. (Most often, this is not the case. They really do love you, they just have a difficult time communicating that love.) You conclude, if my own parents can't even love me, I must not be lovable. This conclusion is reinforced by your friends at school who reject you from time to time. Then you come to Jesus to save you from your sins and make you right with God. But you bring the mentality that you aren't lovable. Someone who feels this way is often not confident about his relationship with God.

The truth is God does love you. He loves you unconditionally. When you realize this you will overcome many of your struggles about your salvation and will rest in the assurance that you really are a Christian.

Q. *Why does God love me so much?*

A. Great question! We often wonder about that after we've really blown it. Like coming home after a rotten day at school, slamming the door, screaming at your parents, smashing your little brother's face into his ice cream bowl and then yelling after stumping your big toe. Then you remember that Jesus has been with you the whole time and you wonder, *Lord, why do You love me so much?*

He loves you because He created you. Have you ever watched a mother and father ooh and ahh over their new-born baby? New-born babies can be just about the ugliest creatures on earth. But not to the parents. They think their baby is the greatest. Why? Because they created the little critter. God loves you because He created you. He thinks you are the greatest.

But more than that, He loves you not because you are lovable, but because He is a God of love. It is His character to love. And there is nothing you can do to make Him stop loving you.

Q. *How can God keep loving me after I've sinned so much?*

A. Imagine it's Halloween night and you go out with your friends, get rowdy and trash the school, costing hundreds of thousands of dollars. Now your friends might applaud your efforts. But God probably wouldn't be quite as excited. Would He quit loving you? No. Nothing you could do would keep Him from continuing in His love for you. Jesus Christ's death on the cross has paid for your sin—past, present and future. That's how much Christ's death for you was worth. Psalm 103:12 says, "As far as the east is from the west, So far has He removed our transgressions from us." He loves you so much that had you been the only person on earth, He would still have left His heavenly home and come down to earth and paid the supreme sacrifice just for you.

Q. *Is there anything that could cause God to change His mind and stop loving me?*

A. We'll let God speak for Himself on that one. Romans 5:8 tells you how much God loved you when you weren't even a Christian: "But God demonstrates His own love toward us, in that while we were yet sinners, Christ died for us." Romans 8:38, 39 tells you what might try to separate you from God's love but can't: "For I am convinced that neither death, nor life, nor angels, nor principalities, nor things present, nor things to come, nor powers, nor height, nor depth, nor any other created thing, shall be able to separate us from the love of God, which is in Christ Jesus our Lord." Jeremiah 31:3 tells you how long God's love will last: "The Lord appeared to him from afar, saying, 'I have loved you with an everlasting love; Therefore I have drawn you with lovingkindness.'"

Get it in your head and don't forget it—*God loves you*. You are special to Him.

Q. *Am I important to God?*

A. What do people do for important people? They honor them, protect them and make special arrangements for them.

God does those exact three things for you. He honors you. Psalm 8:4, 5 says, "What is man, that Thou dost take thought of him? And the son of man, that Thou dost care for him? Yet Thou hast made him a little lower than God, And dost crown him with glory and majesty!" He has sent His angels to guard you. Psalm 91:11 says, "For He will give His angels charge concerning you, to guard you in all your ways." And he is making special arrangements for you. John 14:2 says, "In My Father's house are many dwelling places; if it were not so, I would have told you; for I go to prepare a place for you."

You are very important to God.

Q. *When God looks at me, what does He see?*

A. To see yourself as God sees you, as you really are, you must understand your position in Christ. Having this proper view of yourself is important in developing a healthy self-image.

These truths about you are found in Ephesians 1:

You are blessed with every spiritual blessing in the heavenly places (v. 3).

You were chosen before the foundation of the world that you should be holy and blameless before Him (v. 4).

You were predestined to adoption as sons (v. 5).

You were redeemed through His blood (v. 7).
You are sealed in Him with the Holy Spirit (v. 13).

Because of your position in Christ, great things are true of you, truths that Paul wants you to know. He therefore prays that the eyes of your heart may be enlightened, so you may know what is the hope of His calling, what are the riches of the glory of His inheritance in the saints, and what is the surpassing greatness of His power toward you who believe (vv. 18, 19). God is concerned that you see yourself as He sees you.

To the positional truths of Ephesians 1 we can add further descriptions of believers after they trust Christ (Eph. 2:4–10). Christians are described as:

- alive together with Christ;
- raised up with Christ;
- seated with Him in the heavenly places;
- in Christ Jesus;
- saved by grace;
- His workmanship.

To appreciate even more what it means to be in Christ, compare the above with the following description of persons before they trust Christ (Eph. 2:1–3). You were:

- dead in trespasses and sins;
- walking according to the prince of the power of this world;
- walking according to the prince of the power of the air;
- walking according to the spirit that is now working in the sons of disobedience;

- living in the lusts of the flesh and of the mind;
- by nature children of wrath.

If you are a believer, however, you can say the following about yourself:

I have peace with God (Rom. 5:1).
I am accepted by God (Eph. 1).
I am a child of God (John 1:12).
I am indwelt by the Holy Spirit (1 Cor. 3:16).
I have access to God's wisdom (James 1:5).
I am helped by God (Heb. 4:16).
I am reconciled to God (Rom. 5:11).
I have no condemnation (Rom. 8:1).
I am justified (Rom. 5:1).
I have His righteousness (Rom. 5:19; 2 Cor. 5:21).
I am His representative (2 Cor. 5:20).
I am completely forgiven (Col. 1:14).
I have my needs met by God (Phil. 4:19).
I am tenderly loved (Jer. 31:3).
I am the aroma of Christ to God (2 Cor. 2:15).
I am a temple of God (1 Cor. 3:16).
I am blameless and beyond reproach (Col. 1:22).

Are you beginning to understand from the above what Paul meant when he emphasized, "Therefore, if anyone is in Christ, he is a new creation; the old has gone, the new has come!"?

When God looks at you, He sees someone who is absolutely awesome (adapted from *His Image . . . My Image*, pp. 100–101).

Q. *God loves everybody. Why should I think I'm anyone special?*

A. You are special because you are a unique individual. Each one of us is a one of a kind. There is no one in the past, present or future who will ever be exactly like you. God loves you for you. That makes you special.

Q. How can God accept me?

A. God can accept you because of what Jesus Christ has done on your behalf. He died for your sins, taking away any and every offense that might come between you and God.

A better question is, "How can God not accept you?" Have you ever thought about it that way? If you are a Christian, you are a child of God. John 1:12 says, "But as many as received Him, to them He gave the right to become children of God, even to those who believe in His name." God is not like many earthly fathers who may consciously or unconsciously reject their children. He is the perfect Father. Because you are God's child He will always accept you. For God to reject you after you have become His child would be worse than returning for homecoming after graduating from school and cheering for the other team.

Q. How can I possibly do everything expected of me in the Bible?

A. First, realize you are His child. So the instruction His Word gives you is not to weigh you down, work you over or wear you down.

Rather, it serves to protect you from harm and provide you with God's best.

Remember going to the dentist as a kid? You probably thought your mom hated you for subjecting you to that mean old man and his array of torturing devices. But now having followed their instructions your teeth aren't falling out of your head from decay. God loves you and gives His Word to guide you and guard you.

Secondly, realize who lives inside you. The Bible has a lot to say about your relationship to the Holy Spirit. As a Christian you have been born of the Spirit (John 3:3–5). The Spirit lives within you (John 14:17) and will be with you forever (John 14:16). The Spirit teaches you what you need to know (John 14:26) and testifies to you that you belong, that you are God's child (Rom. 8:16). He guides you (Rom. 8:14) and provides for you the talents, abilities and spiritual gifts that you need to live a purposeful life serving God (1 Cor. 12:4, 11). The Spirit helps you in your weakness and intercedes for you (Rom. 8:26, 27).

The most effective way to grasp the potential competence you have through the Holy Spirit is to understand the resources available to you as a result of the Spirit's indwelling presence (adapted from *His Image . . . My Image*, pp. 111, 112).

Q. Why can't I do things as well as other people?

A. God has given some people strengths that He hasn't given to others. Not everyone is the school jock, the school brain or the campus sweetheart. Not everyone can meet people easily or serve as club president. God did this intentionally.

But He didn't leave you out! God has given each one of His children certain gifts. First Peter 4:10–11 says, "As each one has received a special gift, employ it in serving one another, as good stewards of the manifold grace of God. Whoever speaks, let him speak, as it were, the utterances of God; whoever serves, let him do so as by the strength which God supplies; so that in all things God may be glorified through Jesus Christ, to whom belongs the glory and dominion forever and ever. Amen." You may not be able to do some things as well as others. But because of the gift God has given you, there are some things you can do better than most. These varieties of strengths cause us to depend on one another. No one person has them all.

Find out what strengths God has given you and use them to serve your church and impact your campus.

Q. *How can someone like me ever be a success in life?*

A. Suppose you needed transportation to school each day. So your dad buys you a brand new BMW that has a gold plated dash. It impresses all your friends so much they fall over dead when they see it.

Trouble is, it won't run. Are you pleased? No way! You're embarrassed because you look like Fred Flintstone as you use your legs to push the car.

The most important thing about anything is its purpose. Something is considered a success if, and only if, it accomplishes its purpose.

Your purpose in life is to glorify God. How? John 15:8 says, "By this is My Father glorified, that you bear much fruit, and so prove to be My disciples." You find this fruit in Galatians 5:22, 23. "But the fruit of the Spirit is love, joy, peace, patience, kindness, goodness, faithfulness, gentleness, self-control; against such things there is no law."

What you do outwardly is not nearly as important to

God as who you are inwardly. Through the Holy Spirit, everyone can develop the character qualities found in Galatians 5:22, 23. To the degree you personally develop those qualities, to that extent you will be a success in life.

Q.   Does God consider me a failure when I sin?

A.   Neither His love nor His view of you changes. What does happen is that your sin grieves God. It's the same feeling you have when your best friend does or says something that hurts you, like forgetting your birthday. (This is not to say God is a pouter.)

What restores your relationship with your best friend is this: they come back and ask your forgiveness. First John 1:9 says, "If we confess our sins, He is faithful and righteous to forgive us our sins and to cleanse us from all unrighteousness." When you do blow it in your relationship with God, get things right with Him ASAP. He loves you too much. Don't put it off.

Q.   How can God forgive me when I can't forgive myself?

A.   To have a healthy self-image, you must see yourself as God does—forgiven. Not to forgive yourself will immobilize you from moving out in life as you walk with God.

An inability to forgive yourself comes from a lack of understanding of what Christ did on the cross. To say that you can't forgive yourself implies either Christ did not die for all your sins, or the brutal death that He suffered for you was not enough to pay for your sin, or what you think about your forgiveness is more important than what God says about it. None of these could possibly be true.

Don't live your life based on a lie. Base it on the truth. Romans 8:1 says, "There is therefore now no condemnation for those who are in Christ Jesus." That's the truth. Believe and receive it. Rejoice in your forgiveness and move on.

Q. *Why do I feel inferior?*

A. Because you don't realize who you are as a Christian. When you do, you will not struggle with an inferiority complex. If anything, you will struggle with an attitude of superiority.

Try to comprehend the meaning of these verses, Ephesians 2:4–6, especially verse six. "But God, being rich in mercy, because of His great love with which He loved us, even when we were dead in our transgressions, made us alive together with Christ (by grace you have been saved), and raised us up with Him, and seated us with Him in the heavenly places, in Christ Jesus."

Imagine yourself, right now, seated beside Jesus Christ up in heaven. (That's like attending the Super Bowl and getting to sit by Joe Montana—at his invitation.) You are the envy of all creation. A Christian need never struggle with inferiority. Not only are you seated beside Christ in heaven, but you are royalty. You are a child of the King. You are a young prince or princess. Remember last homecoming how your school's homecoming queen regally paraded across the football field? The day before she may have walked the way Charlie Chaplin did in the old silent movies. But the day she realized she was queen, she walked like a queen.

When you accept that you are a prince or princess, you, too, can walk, act and feel like royalty. By accepting your new position in Christ you move into a whole new dimension of life.

Q. *What if I have a physical deformity?*

A. If possible you can change it, especially if it keeps you from accomplishing what God has called you to do. For example, if you have crooked teeth, get braces. If you have a wart on the end of your nose so big that your eyes cross, have it removed.

But if you can't change it, then you need to accept it as from the hand of your gracious and loving heavenly Father. To make it easier to accept (and in some situations, it won't be easy), remember that God puts prime importance on what qualities are in your life, not what you look like or can accomplish. First Samuel 16:7 says, "But the Lord said to Samuel, 'Do not look at his appearance or at the height of his stature, because I have rejected him; for God sees not as man sees, for man looks at the outward appearance, but the Lord looks at the heart.'" If you have a physical defect, deformity or handicap, use it to become a better person (more like Christ), not a bitter person (one filled with anger and resentment because of your condition).

Q. *Isn't it wrong to love myself?*

A. Have you ever watched the guys at school who have to look at themselves every time they pass by a mirror or a glass window where they can see their reflection? Makes you sick to see them primping, huh? Especially when they start to flex.

God isn't too fired up about that kind of self-love. God calls that conceit.

But God does want you to love yourself. Matthew 22:39 says, "The second is like it, 'You shall love your neighbor as yourself.'" This kind of self-love means that you see yourself as God sees you, someone who is loved, valued and accepted. When you love yourself in this manner it's not just okay, it is what God desires.

Q. Isn't a healthy self-image the same as pride?

A. It can be. Keep in mind, however, there are two types of self-images. When you see yourself as God sees you, you have a healthy self-image. A healthy self-image is very positive. Yet it is very humble because it recognizes its source—the Lord Jesus Christ.

The second type of self-image is an unhealthy self-image. People who have an unhealthy self-image can be divided into two groups: negative and positive. Those with a negative self-image think poorly about themselves. Those with a healthy self-image think good of themselves. But their self-worth is based on the world's system: looks, abilities, intelligence and the like. When people think well about themselves based on the world's system, they may very well struggle with pride.

Q. Isn't having a healthy self-image the same thing as positive thinking? You know, something like, "If I think I will succeed, I will succeed."

A. There is something to be said for positive thinking. You will never get anywhere in life thinking negatively. Thinking positively can draw out the potential in a person. But positive thinking can never produce things that don't already exist. Consider the following story.

Some parents were having trouble with their twin boys. One was abnormally happy all the time while the other was eternally depressed. The parents decided that it was time to seek professional help.

A psychiatrist claimed to have the cure for this family dilemma. He took the happy boy and placed him in a room filled with horse manure and a pitchfork. Figuring that this would cure him from his joyful spirit, the doctor shouted, "Dig," and then left.

Then they took the pessimist and placed him in a room filled with toys and candy. He was free to play with it all. "That should cure him!" exclaimed the psychiatrist. "We'll come back in a few hours and see how he fared."

Upon returning, the parents and the doctor visited the little pessimist. They were shocked to see the little fellow sobbing in the middle of the floor. "I might hurt myself if I play with these toys!" cried the unchanged child.

"Well, your other boy will be cured," the doctor said as he tried to look confident. Peering into the room, the adults were astounded to see the optimist pitching manure in a fury. The mother tried to get the boy to slow down, but he was so busy that he only paused to say, "With all this manure, there must be a pony in here somewhere!"

If you think negatively, you will never have a healthy self-image. But as you believe God's Word about what He says concerning you as His special child, you will discover gifts God has prepared for you that far surpass the excitement of a pony.

Q. How can I begin to see myself as God sees me?

A. The quickest and surest way to discover who you really are is to spend time meditating on God's Word. That doesn't mean to sit on top of a Bible with your legs crossed as you hum and breathe incense. It does mean you read God's Word until you find a verse or passage of scripture that speaks about who you are or how you are feeling. Once you find a verse like that, you think about it and pray about it until it becomes real in your experience. John 8:31, 32 says, "Jesus therefore was saying to those Jews who had believed Him, 'If you abide in My word, then you are truly disciples of Mine; and you shall know the truth, and the truth shall make you free.'"

For example, if you struggle with the following, meditate on the passages of scripture beside it so the truth in the last column will become yours:

How I feel	*Scripture*	*What is really true*
Unacceptable	Rom. 15:7	Accepted
Inadequate	Phil. 4:13	Can do all things
Fearful	Isa. 41:10	Supported by God Himself
Insecure	Prov. 3:25, 26	Confident
Unloved	Eph. 3:17–19	Loved

A great project to get you started is to read through the Book of Ephesians, listing everything that is true of a Christian. When you finish your list, each day choose one of the truths to pray and think about.

Q. How should I respond when people cut me down or criticize me?

A. Many a guy has lost confidence in his athletic ability when a friend laughed at his idea to go out for a certain sport, say baseball. Comments like, "You are so uncoordinated, you couldn't catch a ball if they rolled it to you." Or take the group of girls who laugh at the new outfit you wear to school. Suddenly you become insecure and can begin doubting your ability to ever dress "correctly."

Criticism can hurt and it can cause potential damage to your self-image if you don't respond to it properly.

God wants you to use these times as opportunities to grow. Proverbs 19:20 says, "Listen to counsel and accept discipline, that you may be wise the rest of your days." When criticized, first see if the complaint is deserved. If it is, then work on changing the situation. Otherwise you will never reach the full potential that God desires for you. Criticism often serves to correct character qualities, change motivations and make you more sensitive to others.

Second, express your appreciation for your friend's input. But avoid being sarcastic like, "Thank you, I value very highly the opinion of a jerk."

Third, remember who you are—God's beloved, holy child. You are valued, accepted and gifted. Don't let the criticism damage that view of yourself. Simply use it to release more fully the potential God has given you.

Q. How should I respond when someone compliments me?

A. Often we go to two extremes, both as a result of pride. One extreme is false humility. We deny any positive quality or accomplishment by saying things like, "No, no, no. I'm just a worm." That makes people sick. Everyone knows you are really saying, "Keep trying to convince me. I'm loving it."

The other extreme is to agree with them to the point of bragging. You know the type. You compliment such people on one thing and they remind you of twenty other things they did well. Yuck.

When you receive a compliment, first see if it is deserved. If it isn't, pass the credit on to someone else. If it is deserved, then simply say, "Thank you." There is nothing at all wrong with accepting a compliment.

Once you receive it, however, pass the praise on to the Lord Jesus Christ. He is the Source of your gifts, abilities, looks, talents and personality. If you hold on to the compliments instead of giving praise to Jesus, you may forget that Christ is Your source and may believe that you are the source. Pride soon develops and can cause terrible consequences. Check out 2 Chronicles 26:3–5, 8, 15–16, and 20–21 for details on what happened to one man who became proud by refusing to pass on praise to the Lord.

Q. *Why am I so frustrated with who I am?*

A. Although God thinks you are the greatest, you may often be reminded by your shortcomings that you have not completely "arrived" yet. You probably experience this most at home where it is the hardest to live out your Christian beliefs. You come home from school and invariably yell at your mom. You retreat back to your room wondering why in the world did you ever respond like that.

Realize that you are growing and maturing in your walk with the Lord. Sure, no one grows as quickly as he wants to grow, but you are growing just the same. Think back over how much Christ has changed you since you invited Him into your heart. And He's not going to stop changing you either. Philippians 1:6 says, "For I am confident of this very thing, that He who began a good work in you will perfect it until the day of Christ Jesus."

Q. *What's the difference in self-acceptance and self-improvement?*

A. Many consider the rose the crowning achievement of God's work in the flower kingdom. All the other flowers are beautiful, but the rose outdoes them all. But a rose left to itself never reaches its fullest potential. It remains small and has lots of thorns. As a gardener tends to it, it improves. It becomes all it is capable of becoming.

In the same way, you are perfect just like you are. But you haven't reached your fullest potential. There are some things you can do in cooperation with God to become all you're capable of becoming.

These don't increase your self-worth, but they do enhance your potential to serve Christ in greater ways than you've ever dreamed. Consider the following:

1. Do not label yourself negatively ("I am stupid" and so on). You tend to become the label you give yourself.
2. When you fail, admit or confess it to God, your Father, and then refuse to condemn yourself.
3. Be as kind to yourself as you would be (or would hope to be) to any other person.
4. Do not compare yourself with others. You are a unique person. God enjoys you in your uniqueness; have a similar attitude toward yourself.
5. Concentrate and meditate on God's grace, love

and acceptance—not on criticisms from other people.

6. Associate with friends who are positive, who delight in you.

7. Start helping others to see themselves as God sees them . . . by accepting them, loving them, and encouraging them.

8. Learn to laugh; look for the humor in life and experience it.

9. Be positive (Phil. 4:8). See how long you can go without saying something negative about another person or situation.

10. List the things you can change, what you will change, how you will change, and when you will change.

11. List the things you would like to change but can't. List their benefits to you.

12. Look your best (grooming, dress, etc.).

13. Take care of yourself by getting proper rest, nutrition, and exercise.

14. Use and develop your talents, i.e., playing the piano, woodworking, etc.

15. Develop your God-given ministry.

(adapted from *His Image . . . My Image*, pp. 163, 164.)

Q. Is having a healthy self-image an end in itself? What do I do once I see and believe who I am from God's perspective?

A. Having a healthy self-image is not an end in itself any more than getting a date is an end in itself. Once you get a date, you want to make the other person feel special.

Once you realize who you are as a follower of Jesus Christ, you will make it your aim to make others feel special. Remember Matthew 22:39? It says, "The second (commandment) is like it, 'You shall love your neighbor as yourself.'"

The goal of learning to like yourself is legitimate only when you love others more as a result. This should be your motivation.

When loving others becomes your desire, everything then falls into place and makes sense. Now others (beginning with Christ) and not yourself are at the center of your attention. And when this happens, God is pleased (adapted from *Self-Image: Learning to Like Yourself*, p. 60).

3   *Peer Pressure*

Q.   *What is peer pressure?*

A. School starts in about ten minutes so you figure it's about time to roll out of bed and get ready. You look in your closet and pull out a black shirt, black pants and black belt, black socks and black shoes. You hurry into the bathroom where you put two cans of mousse in your hair, then part it just above your left ear and brush it all over to the other side of your head. You take one last glance in the mirror. *Perfect.* As you race through the kitchen you bump into Mom. She takes one look at you and screams. Near hysteria, she raves about the way you look.

Undisturbed (you've been through this so many times before) you tell her, "But Mom, this is how all my friends dress." As if that were the ultimate answer to all mankind's questions.

As you jump in the car you ask yourself,

"Why am I dressed this way? It's the dumbest look-ing outfit I've ever worn!"

Why do you wear it? Peer pressure. Peer pressure is that powerful influence your friends have over you that dictates the clothes you wear, the words you use, the people you associate with, the places you go and the attitude you have. It is the pressure you experience to conform to the standards of your friends even if you don't want to. It can be either good or bad, depending on where your friends are coming from.

In the 1960s the most powerful influence in a teenager's life was his parents, followed by teachers and then his peers. But in the 1980s peer pressure ranked first, followed by parents and then the media (adapted from *Teenage Morality Study*, p. 25, Josh McDowell Ministry).

Q. Why is peer pressure so powerful?

A. You have just come home from school, and you can hold back the tears no longer. Over and over you hear your best friend's comment, "You wore those jeans last week. Don't you have anything else to wear? Besides, jeans like that have been out of style for six months."

Your heart hurts so much you think you will die. You purpose that whatever it takes, whether you have to beg, borrow or steal, you will have acquired a new pair of jeans by tomorrow morning.

Peer pressure is so powerful because every single person on earth has a God-given need to be loved and accepted. God wants you to find this drive fulfilled in your love-relationship with Himself. He wants you to be secure in how much He loves and accepts you as His chosen child. If you aren't, you will look to your friends for acceptance. The greater your insecurity, the greater your need for acceptance and the more significant the opinions of your friends become. For some, a friend's opinion becomes the driving force of life.

Q. Do parents understand how tough it is to put up with peer pressure day after day, after day?

A. It's not like peer pressure didn't exist during cavemen times when they were going through school. But the intensity of pressure just wasn't the same. Your dad being pressured to smoke a cigarette out in the school parking lot is nothing compared to the pressure on you to smoke crack. Nor can your mom's one experience with her boyfriend wanting to take her parking compare to the pressure you get to go all the way because it's the "in" thing to do today. Because the intensity levels are light years apart, some parents find it hard to understand.

Q. *My girlfriends at school keep making fun of me because I'm still a virgin. What can I do?*

A. What would you guess is the number one pressure on a girl to become sexually active? If you guessed guys, you're wrong. The greatest pressure often comes from her own girlfriends. If you find yourself in a situation like this, remember there are some things that you can give away only once. And your virginity is one of them. Don't sacrifice, like so many women do, the things that are eternal on the altar of the immediate. That is, don't give away something you can never give away again to some guy (who buys you a lousy hamburger and takes you to see a movie you have already seen before), just because your girlfriends are pressuring you. The next time they begin to hassle you, you might want to tell them what one young lady told her friends. "In five minutes, I can become like you. But try as hard as you can, you can never again become like me."

Q. *Why shouldn't I mess around with my girlfriend? My friends all tell me "It's natural."*

A. It's also natural to burp in public, or to run around naked. But do you do that? No. Not everything that is natural is proper. Some things offend others. And to mess around with your girlfriend, even if she wants to, offends other people.

Consider the effect your actions would have on her parents if they ever found out. Or on her future husband. Or what about her future children? Your actions would hurt them deeply. What are you going to tell her dad when he comes banging on your front door with one hand, carrying a baseball bat in the other? "But, sir, it's the natural thing to do"?

When the guys pressure you with the "It's natural" thing again, tell them to go pick their noses. It's natural. Besides, it should keep them entertained for a while.

Q. My boyfriend keeps telling me if I loved him, I would let him. I don't know if I can resist much longer. What should I do?

A. When the Bible talks about love, the first characteristic it mentions is patience. First Corinthians 13:4 says, "Love is patient." Real love can always wait to give. Lust, however, is different. Whereas love can always wait to give it, lust can never wait to get it. It sounds like your boyfriend has confused lust for love. He is pressuring you to get something that if he really loved you, he would wait for.

You don't have to put up with the pressure. Tell him that if he really loved you, he would wait. That puts the pressure back on him—where it belongs.

Q. My girlfriend wants for us to make love together. I told her "no," but she says one time won't hurt. What do I tell her?

A. We've already mentioned that it only takes one time

(the first time) to lose your virginity. But do you know how many times it takes to get pregnant? Once. Many kids think a girl can't get pregnant the first time. But that's an old wives' tale.

But think about this also. How many times does it take to catch a disease like herpes, gonorrhea or even AIDS? One time and one time only. You are not immune. There are fifty-one sexually transmitted diseases. Two and one half million teenagers will get one of these diseases this year. Did you know that more school-aged kids have gonorrhea than combined cases of rubella, mumps, measles and chicken pox!

Look at the diagram on page 72. Say one of you have messed around before, with two other people. And let's say that each of these have also messed around with two other people. In today's society or even in the church, that would not be at all unusual. Notice how the multiplication of partners grows and grows and grows as you trace back the "sexual activity family tree."

If any one of these people tested HIV positive (that is, were carrying the AIDS producing virus), everyone of the people who are connected could possibly be carrying that virus. The only way to know is either to go get tested or wait for a few years until the virus begins to manifest its deadly effects.

An example of the multiplication effect is reported by the Centers for Disease Control in Atlanta: "A 16-year-old girl was responsible for 218 cases of syphilis and 440 cases of gonorrhea. Here is what happened: The girl had sex with 16 men and sex with other people who had sex with other people. The number of contacts finally added up to 1,660. . . . What if the girl had had AIDS, instead of gonorrhea and syphilis? You probably would

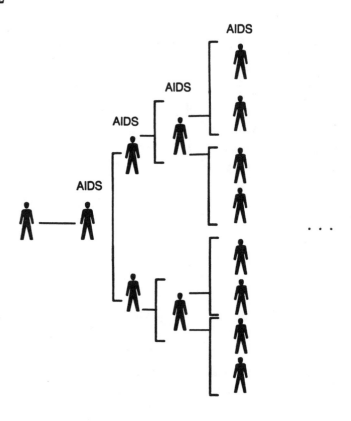

have had 1,000 dead people by now" (*The Common Appeal*, Friday 11/7/88, p. A12).

Q. *My boyfriend says we will be okay because we will use protection. Would we really be safe?*

A. No form of birth control is 100 percent effective, not even the pill.

The form of protection that guys commonly use is as safe statistically as playing Russian roulette. It has been said that Russian roulette was a game developed by soldiers who had given up hope and had nothing else better to do than to put one bullet into the chamber of a gun, leaving the other five chambers empty. They would then spin the chamber, not knowing if the bullet lined up with the trigger. Then they would pull the trigger. They had a 5 in 6 or 83 percent chance of living. That's a pretty good chance. Odds are they would walk away okay from their little game. If you had to bet, then the best bet would be on the guy to live.

When a guy uses protection, there's about an 85 percent chance it will work. Again, those are pretty good odds if you have to bet. But think of the down side. Sometimes, when you play the game, the gun goes off.

Why play with your life and future when you don't have to? The only safe approach to sex is to follow God's instructions of waiting until marriage. The only way to avoid risks is not to have intercourse.

Q. What do I do when my girlfriend wants me to mess around with her? She says we don't have to go all the way.

A. You may not go all the way the first time, or even the second. But once you start messing around, it takes more and more to satisfy you. Soon there is nothing else to do but go all the way.

The Bible is clear that we are wrong when we transgress God's laws. When you "just mess around," it causes the one you are with, and yourself, to want to go all the way. Going all the way is meant for after marriage. So when you cause someone to do something that is meant only for marriage, we believe you have transgressed (1 Thess. 44:4).

Tell your girlfriend that the best way to control yourselves is not even to get started.

Q. But what if my boyfriend and I are going to get married?

A. A wedding ring doesn't make you a pure person. (Only Jesus Christ working in a dynamic way in your life can make you pure.) So if you are impure before your wedding day, you'll be impure after your wedding day. The same with your boyfriend. If he is impure before, he will be impure afterwards. And how much can you trust a marriage partner when you know he struggles with moral impurity? You can't.

Q. My girlfriend wants to make sure we are sexually compatible before we get married. Is that legitimate?

A. You don't buy a brand new pair of shoes without first trying them on, do you? Of course not! So then it makes sense to make sure you are sexually compatible before you are married, right? *Wrong!*

In the first place, neither one of you is a pair of shoes. You are not taking something home to try on or use. If you want to compare your wedding night to something, a better analogy would be giving a box of Kleenex to somebody. No matter how pretty the color, how much would they appreciate it if they discovered the Kleenex had been used? God has designed your wedding night to be like the explosion of dynamite. If you don't wait, it can be reduced to nothing more than the pop of a little firecracker.

Rarely will you find two people who aren't sexually compatible. So tell your girlfriend you are waiting for the fireworks.

Q. My boyfriend keeps telling me to trust him. Should I?

A. Guys have had a proverb that goes back to the beginning of time. "Tell a girl what she wants to hear and you have what you want to have." Guys know that saying the right words like, "I love you," "You are the only one I have ever really cared for," or "You're the most beautiful girl in the whole world," can get a girl's emotions going crazy. You hear those words and get attacked by a severe case of the "fuzzy-wuzzies." Then while you're vulnerable, he makes his moves.

If your boyfriend is constantly having to convince you that he is trustworthy, chances are he isn't. Be careful of dropping your guard even for a moment, regardless of what someone says. What's most important is how he acts, not what he says. When it comes to trust, actions speak much louder than words.

Q. *All my friends have started drinking and want me to join them. I turn eighteen next month. Is it wrong for me to join them?*

A. Just because something is legal doesn't make it right, like abortion for example. What makes something right is what God's Word has to say about it.

Check out what the Bible has to say about drinking:

> Leviticus 10:8–11, "The Lord then spoke to Aaron, saying, 'Do not drink wine or strong drink, neither you nor your sons with you, when you come into the tent of meeting, so that you may not die—it is a perpetual statute throughout your generations—and so as to make a distinction between the holy and the profane, and between the unclean and the clean, and so as to teach the sons of Israel all the statutes which the Lord has spoken to them through Moses.'"

Proverbs 20:1, "Wine is a mocker, strong drink a brawler, And whoever is intoxicated by it is not wise."

Proverbs 21:17, "He who loves pleasure will become a poor man; He who loves wine and oil will not become rich."

Proverbs 23:29–35, "Who has woe? Who has sorrow? Who has contentions? Who has complaining? Who has wounds without cause? Who has redness of eyes? Those who linger long over wine, those who go to taste mixed wine. Do not look on the wine when it is red, When it sparkles in the cup, When it goes down smoothly; At the last it bites like a serpent, And stings like a viper. Your eyes will see strange things, And your mind will utter perverse things. And you will be like one who lies down in the middle of the sea, Or like one who lies down on the top of a mast, 'They struck me, but I did not become ill; They beat me, but I did not know it. When shall I awake? I will seek another drink.'"

Romans 13:13, "Let us behave properly as in the day, not in carousing and drunkenness, not in sexual promiscuity and sensuality, not in strife and jealousy."

Galatians 5:21, "Envying, drunkenness, carousing, and things like these, of which I forewarn you just as I have forewarned you that those who practice such things shall not inherit the kingdom of God."

If your friends pressure you with, "Come on, everybody's doing it," you tell them everybody but you. Don't be afraid to be different. God is against the misuse of alcohol. Stand up for what is right.

Q. My friends keep teasing me because I don't drink. They ask me what I am afraid of. What can I tell them to make them back off?

A. Tell them it's not because of fear that you don't drink. Tell them it's because you are smart. Proverbs 22:3, 5 says, "The prudent sees the evil and hides himself, But the naive go on, and are punished for it. Thorns and snares are in the way of the perverse; He who guards himself will be far from them."

Just because all your friends are doing something doesn't mean it's a wise thing for you to do. Alcoholism is America's third largest health problem, following heart disease and cancer.

It affects ten million people, costs sixty billion dollars, and is implicated in two hundred thousand deaths annually. Alcohol is involved in 50 percent of deaths by motor vehicle and fire, 67 percent of murders, and 33 percent of suicides.

It contributes to morbidity in certain malignancies and to many diseases of the endocrine, cardiovascular, gastrointestinal and nervous systems.

The suicide rate of alcoholics has been found to be six to twenty times higher than that of the general population.

With this damaging evidence, if alcohol were to be presented for legalization as a drug today, it surely would not be accepted (adapted from *Hot Topics* by Bill Myers, pp. 81–82).

Physically alcohol can damage your liver, put undue stress on your heart and impair your memory. Emotionally it can cause you embarrassment from stupid behavior and create anxiety, cause family hassles, guilt from improper actions and a poor self-image. What happens is, that alcohol limits your freedom. It limits your ability to make *right* decisions and to act upon them. Don't give in to your friends' pressure. Hold firm. They will probably continue to tease you. But know that deep down they respect you for your convictions.

Q. My friends complain I'm too shy. They think I should go out drinking with them. They say it will loosen me up. I would like to be a little more outgoing. What should I do?

A. If you want a personality makeover, drinking will do that for you. Some shy people become the life of the party once they get drunk. Others try to kill themselves.

If you are really in search of a personality makeover, read Ephesians 5:18, "And do not get drunk with wine, for that is dissipation, but be filled with the Spirit." When you come under the influence of either alcohol or the Holy Spirit, you will act differently. You may not know how alcohol will make you act, but you do know how the Holy Spirit will make you act—just like Jesus. Instead of giving in to your friends' pressure to drink, give in to the Spirit's promptings in your life. Let Him control you, lead you and empower you. Your friends will be shocked to see the new you.

Q. My friends tell me if I want to be popular I need to drink. Is that true?

A. Here's a radical statement. Popularity isn't everything. Drinking may make you popular with your friends now. But what if they next decide that popping a few pills is what it takes to be popular? Is it worth it? At some point you have to draw a line that you refuse to cross. Why not draw that line now? It may make you unpopular for a while with the group you hang around with now. The Bible says that God is constantly looking for guys and gals who are completely sold out to Him. Second Chronicles 16:9 says, "For the eyes of the Lord move to and fro throughout the earth that He may strongly support those whose heart is completely His." When He finds a person like that He backs him up 100 percent.

In the long run, you will find that it is better to stick to your convictions and be unpopular than to compromise your convictions and be popular. Your friends may reject you at first. But that's okay. If they do, they weren't the greatest of friends to begin with.

Q. My friends pressure me to drink by saying it's just part of growing up. Should I give in and get it over with?

A. Being pressured to drink may be a part of growing up, but drinking doesn't have to be. The church needs more and more students who refuse to give in to the pressure. It *is* possible to go through high school and even college without once compromising.

Your campus needs Christians who have a reputation for being different. The world rarely sees any distinction between Sammy Saved and Larry Lost. Both go to school Monday through Friday. Both go to parties Friday and Saturday. About the only difference is Sammy doesn't get to sleep in on Sunday mornings.

Reputations can be destroyed with one drink. Keep your testimony intact. Tell you friends that you'll stick to the growing up. But you'll leave the throwing up to them.

Q. My friends want to turn me on. I'm scared. I know absolutely nothing about drugs. What does the Bible say about drugs?

A. You almost need a doctorate in pharmacology to keep up with the different kinds of drugs today. Most drugs can be grouped into the following major categories (see chart on p. 81).

Often drugs are used in combination. Some of the most common include: heroin and cocaine ("speed ball"), marijuana and Black Flag Roach Killer ("WACS"), marijuana and cocaine ("sherm"), marijuana and PCP ("embalming fluid").

Since statistics show that one out of four students ages 13–17 have been offered illegal drugs in the past 30 days (*USA Today,* 8/15/89, p. 1), it's not surprising that you have friends pressuring you to turn on.

The Bible doesn't speak to the subject of drug abuse directly. But it doesn't talk about which side of the expressway to drive on either. The Bible does say that your body is God's temple. First Corinthians 3:16, 17 says, "Do you not know that you are a temple of God, and that the Spirit of God dwells in you? If any man destroys the temple of God, God will destroy him, for the temple of God is holy, and that is what you are."

Drug abuse does nothing positive for your body. If anything, it is destructive. Whatever you do, don't subject your body, God's temple, to the degrading effects of drugs.

Q. But my friends say I don't know what I'm missing. The way they talk I'm missing a great experience. Is getting high that big of a deal?

A. Not doing drugs causes you to miss a lot, a whole lot! Just look at all the fun things listed on page 82 that you don't get to experience:

Category	Types	Street Names	Common Usage	Experience
Cannabis	Marijuana Hashish	Joint, grass, pot, toke, reefer, roach, weed, dope, hash	Smoke	Euphoria, hallucinations
Depressants	Barbiturates Valium Quaaludes	Downers, barbs, yellow jackets, red devils, blue devils	Swallow	Intoxication, relaxation, calm tension, relieve anxiety
Stimulants	Amphetamines Diet pills Cocaine Crack	Uppers, speed, crank, crystal, black beauties, pep pills Snow, coke	Swallow or inject	
Hallucinogens	LSD PCP Mescaline	Acid, angel dust, cactus	Sniff, inject, smoke	Brief euphoria, exceptional feeling of well being, followed by depression
Designer Drugs	MDMA	Ecstacy	Swallow, inject	
Inhalants	Glue Gasoline Aerosols Antihistamines	Huff	Inhale	Altered perception & mood
Narcotics	Opium Heroin Morphine Codeine	Junk, smack, horse	Inject, smoke, swallow	

(Adapted from *Help Your Children Say No to Drugs* by John Q. Baucom, pp. 184–187.)

The Drug	"The Fun"
Cannabis	addiction, impaired short memory, panic reaction, depression, anxiety
Depressants	addiction, impaired judgment, drowsiness, confusion, slurred speech, withdrawal more dangerous than withdrawal from heroin, overdose can result in death (greatly increased when taken with alcohol)
Stimulants	irritability, nervousness, paranoia, stay awake for as long as six days but the crash at the end can be devastating, suicidal tendencies, overdoses can result in death
Hallucinogens	PCP can distort reality so much that symptoms resemble mental illness, violent behavior, destructive, some have drowned in shallow ponds or burned to death in fires because PCP actually blocked the pain
Designer Drugs	extremely powerful and very dangerous (example: Fenatyl, a synthetic duplicate of heroin, is a thousand times stronger), death from overdose
Inhalants	impaired judgment, poor coordination, can become abusive and violently dangerous to yourself and others, damages the brain, liver, kidneys and bone marrow, sometimes death from arrhythmia (irregular heartbeat), and death by lack of oxygen
Narcotics	addiction, significant weight loss, hepatitis, AIDS from unsterile needles

(Adapted from Baucom, pp. 184–187.)

But consider this: "There isn't a drug out there that hasn't been cut with something by the time it gets to us. If we're smoking pot we'll probably also be smoking fertilizer. Doing mescaline? Count on a bad batch of LSD with some PCP thrown in for good measure. The list goes on. . . .

"And forget quality control. We're not talking your

sparkling-clean pharmaceutical lab here. We're talking grungy basements or bathrooms. We're talking dealers looking out for the dollars, not for your health.

"Since there is no quality control, you may be doing one drug for months and then, without knowing it, you're doing the same amount but from a batch five times stronger. And then, without knowing it, you get to ride in an ambulance—or a hearse.

"And finally, in the physical department, there are dangers of our own actions while under the influence. Actions such as:

—the high rate of suicides from the depression that follows;

—the fact that one out of every five accidents is drug/alcohol related which, by the way, makes substance abuse the number one killer of teenagers;

—the frightening number of murders and self-mutilations—like the girl who ate her fingers while doing angel dust" (*More Hot Topics*, Bill Myers, pp. 77, 78).

Can't wait to get in on all the fun—right?

Q. My friends tell me to just try it once and see what it's like. What's wrong with a little experimenting?

A. Leave your experiments to chemistry lab. Experimenting leads to addiction.

"Did you know that studies prove that one out of every five who try cocaine for the first time become dependent upon the drug? One out of five!

"And according to the National Institute on Alcohol Abuse and Alcoholism, it is nearly that same percentage of teenagers across America (one out of five) that have become problem drinkers" (Myers, p. 80).

"The evolutionary aspects of drug use are real. There is, beyond any doubt, a predictable progression to drug use. Students almost never experiment with cocaine, heroin, or any of the 'hard' drugs without first using gateway drugs: marijuana, alcohol, and/or tobacco. Two studies found a constant progression of drug abuse among high school students. The pattern consistently followed four well-defined steps:

1. beer or wine
2. hard liquor and/or cigarettes
3. marijuana
4. other illicit drugs

"Researchers reported that virtually no one moves to step four without first going through steps one, two, and three" (Baucom, p. 34).

"Addiction is a biochemical and physiological process by which a person can develop a cellular 'oneness' with a foreign chemical. The substance actually joins with a person's body to the point that to 'feel normal' new supplies of the substance must be consumed. If not replenished, the addict experiences physiological withdrawal symptoms. In many ways the reaction can be as dramatic as if part of the addict's anatomy was amputated. These reactions may also include emotional pain, but are not limited to emotions. Withdrawal can cause a variety of visceral responses, including shaking, chills, sweating, seizures, convulsions, increased heart rate, craving for the drug, and possibly even death. Addiction is deadly and, in fact, the Latin root word 'addictus' means slave" (Baucom, p. 77).

Be smart. Don't see how close you can get to the edge before you fall off. Don't try any drug, even once.

Q. I have a lot of problems. My friends say I should try some stuff to get away from it all. What do you think?

A. Drugs don't make your problems go away. While on a high, you may escape them for a while, but when you come back down, your problems are always there waiting for you.

If anything, drugs only make your problems worse. Now you have all the trouble that drugs bring along with them like the need for extra cash, the need to keep what you do secret, the problems with parents, teachers and the authorities, the tendency to either do drugs more often, in heavier dosages, or move on up the ladder to a stronger drug.

When you get into drugs you also lose your ability to make intelligent, rational decisions and act upon them. You become a slave to a cruel taskmaster. You lose your freedom to decide where you want your life to head. Drugs begin dictating every aspect of your life.

Q. I quit doing drugs, but my friend keeps after me. He says I did it before, what's the big deal now? What should I do?

A. Be careful of the devil's tricks. (This is not to say that your friend is the devil, even though he may act like a demon from time to time.) That crafty ol' snake knows how to really get to Christians. He will play up the fact that you have blown it in the past. Then he will make you think that since you have once dirtied yourself, you will never get the stain out of your life completely. It's a lie! Isaiah 1:18–20 says, "'Come now, and let us reason together,' says the Lord, 'Though your sins are as scarlet, They will be as white as snow; Though they are red like crimson, They will be like wool. If you consent and obey, You will eat the best of the land; But if you refuse and rebel, You will be devoured by the sword.'"

God is the God of the second chance. The third and the fourth and the fifth chance, for that matter. If you have made the break and asked God to forgive you, then you are as white as snow in His eyes (His kind of snow, not the drug kind of snow).

Tell your friends you are different now. Identify yourself with your King—Jesus Christ the Lord. Tell them you've made the break and you aren't going back. Don't be condemning and don't act holier-than-thou. But be firm and confident. Show your friends that they, too, can have hope. Help them find their way out of the mess they're in.

Q. *How can I know if something is right or wrong?*

A. When you wonder if something is right or wrong, ask these questions. They will help you make the right choice:

1. *The Personal Test:* Will doing it make me a better or worse Christian?
2. *The Practical Test:* Will doing it likely bring desirable or undesirable results?
3. *The Social Test:* Will doing it influence others to be better or worse Christians?

4. *The Universal Test:* Suppose everyone did it?
5. *The Scriptural Test:* Is it expressly forbidden in the Word of God?
6. *The Stewardship Test:* Will doing it involve a waste of God's talents invested in me?
7. *The Missionary Test:* Will doing it likely help or hinder the progress of the kingdom of God on earth?
8. *The Character Test:* Will doing it make me stronger or weaker morally?
9. *The Publicity Test:* Would I be willing for my friends to know about it?
10. *The Common Sense Test:* Does it reflect good, everyday, common "horse" sense?
11. *The Family Test:* Will doing it bring credit or dishonor to my family?

Q. Why are the fun things always wrong?

A. God has placed you on planet Earth and has released you to have a great time. He wants you to experience life to its fullest. That's why He's made certain things off limits. He knows not everything is good for you. He knows there are certain play areas where you can get killed.

God isn't down on your fun. Not at all. He wants you to have fun and not regret it. God has placed limits to protect you. He loves you and doesn't want to scrape you up off the pavement somewhere.

Q. What do I do when I know something is wrong, but I still want to do it?

A. Realize that you are in a war. Here is a reconnaissance report:

The Enemy: The devil (a.k.a.: roaring lion, serpent, prince of darkness).

His Strategy: Appeals to the lust of the flesh, lust of eyes and the boastful pride of life to cause you to sin. Expert on deception. Makes temptation look like a good move when actually it is a big rip-off.

His Targeted Victory: To devour the people of God and destroy the kingdom of God. Will stop at nothing to accomplish his objectives (adapted from *Temptation: Avoiding the Big Rip-Off,* p. 36).

One of the devil's primary tactics is to take an activity (whether it's drinking, drugs or "doin' it") and minimize the disadvantages (consequences) while maximizing its advantages (benefits).

When the devil tempts you, ask God for a clear head to think through the worst thing that could happen to you and the best thing that could happen to you if you were to give in. Once you compare the two, you probably won't want to do it as badly anymore. Then ask the Holy Spirit to fill you with His power to make the right choice.

Q. How much should I stand up for my faith at school?

A. Realize it will be tough when you take a stand. People will be watching you. That's why some will tease you, others will give you a hard time if you do the least little thing wrong. But you don't have to pretend you are perfect. When you blow it, admit it, get up and move on. You are a *follower* of Jesus Christ, not Jesus Christ Himself.

Don't let fear of turning your friends off keep you from standing up for your faith. Many may be waiting for someone to just lead the way so they will have a positive role model to pattern their own lives after.

As you stay sensitive to the Holy Spirit's promptings in your life, you'll know when, if necessary, to keep quiet. We aren't saying you need to stand on the table every day and preach the gospel to the students while they eat. But we do encourage you to stand up for what you believe. Who knows what kind of spiritual fire might start from your sparks?

Q. What do I do when people make fun of me for being a Christian?

A. You walk down the hallway with your Love God, Hate Sin t-shirt on. You get some stares but you hardly even notice. It's not till first period class when your friends crack about a hundred jokes concerning your t-shirt, your church and your faith that you think, *Oh, brother, did I goof by letting my youth minister talk me into wearing this t-shirt to school today!*

The next time you get laughed at for being a Christian or get made fun of by your friends because you take a stand not to do something wrong, throw a party! The Bible says you are blessed. Matthew 5:11, 12 says, "Blessed are you when men cast insults at you, and persecute you, and say all kinds of evil against you falsely, on account of Me. Rejoice, and be glad, for your reward in heaven is great, for so they persecuted the prophets who were before you." You may ask, what is there to be happy about? Obviously not the pain and the embarrassment. You can be happy because you have been considered worthy to suffer for the name of Jesus Christ. Acts 5:40, 41 says, "And they took his advice; and after calling the apostles in, they flogged them and ordered them to speak no more in the name of Jesus, and then released them. So they went on their way from the presence of the Council, rejoicing that they had been considered worthy to suffer shame for His name."

Q. *How do I stand up for what I believe without losing my friends?*

A. The quickest way to turn off your peers is by saying, "I'm a good Christian and I don't do those things!" Instead say, "I accept you as you are. Please, accept me as I am," or "I don't drink and I want to keep it that way." If you accept other people just as they are, it is amazing how they'll respond. Usually you'll be accepted and well liked even without participating in all their activities.

But that's not always the case. Sometimes you do lose your friends or you'll enter into a period of loneliness. Be encouraged, however. It is only a transition period.

If it comes down to winning a popularity contest or winning the pleasure of Jesus Christ, go for the latter every time. If your friends reject you because of the stand you've taken, it is really Christ and not you they are rejecting.

Q. *I'm tired of always saying "no." What can I do to keep from giving up?*

A. Picture yourself walking down a road. Everything is going fine. The scenery is beautiful, the weather great. As you round the curve, you see a fork in the road. The road to the right is narrow and goes straight uphill. The road to the left is wide and broad and leads downhill. The right-hand road is the one you should take, but it looks so difficult to travel. The road on the left, however, looks so easy. To make things worse, you see a sign that says:

> Wherever you are going,
> the left-hand road
> will get you there faster.
> Signed,
> Sly

What are you going to do?

Regardless of how hard or long it seems, if you want to honor your Lord, you must take the road on the right, the road that leads away from temptation. Doing this takes faith.

Take sex, for example. Left-hand road thinking says, "Any time, any place, any one." Right-hand road thinking says, "I am confident that if I do not compromise physically, God will build character into my life, provide the right person for me to marry and bless my marriage with a dynamic sex life."

Faith says, "Regardless of what the devil says, regardless of what my body wants, regardless of how quick and easy it seems, regardless of how secret it will be, I choose to act on what God wants me to do."

As you walk the path of life, you will encounter many forks in the road. Each time you must make a choice. The first choice is always the hardest. Each time after that it gets easier.

It's like training for a marathon. The first run is always a killer, but as a runner builds up strength and endurance the runs become easier and he can go farther.

Only after months of training is he ready for a 26.2-mile race.

But what would happen if our marathon runner got lazy and quit training or started eating junk food or began hanging around with people who said running was bad for a person?

Spiritual laziness, spiritual junk food (like watching too much TV when you could be reading your Bible), or hanging around with people opposed to godly things will affect your spiritual endurance (adapted from *Temptation*, HLP, pp. 53–55).

If you want to honor Jesus Christ all the way to the end of the race, then first be a man or woman of faith and second, stay spiritually fit so you will have the endurance to keep saying "no." Isaiah 40:28–31 says, "Do you not know? Have you not heard? The Everlasting God, the Lord, the Creator of the ends of the earth does not become weary or tired. His understanding is inscrutable. He gives strength to the weary, and to him who lacks might He increases power. Though youths grow weary and tired, and vigorous young men stumble badly, Yet those who wait for the Lord will gain new strength; They will mount up with wings like eagles, They will run and not get tired, They will walk and not become weary."

Q. What's the best way for me and my friends to stay out of trouble?

A. One of the best ways is to learn to avoid situations where you know you will be pressured to compromise. Think about it: If you know you will be in a situation, wouldn't it be wiser not to go? (Now don't take this to the extreme and decide that since you may be pressured at school you'd better not go to class!) Romans 13:14 says it this way:

> "But put on the Lord Jesus Christ, and make no provision for the flesh in regard to its lusts."

Some of the most common peer-pressure-packed situations (say that ten times real fast) include certain parties, places, possessions.

For example, going to some kinds of parties is just asking for trouble. The same goes for certain types of places (like your girlfriend's or boyfriend's home when parents are away). Certain possessions, too, can be killers in your walk with Christ (like a six-pack of beer) (adapted from *Peer Pressure*, p. 56).

Turn on your spiritual radar. If you sense you are going to be in a tempting situation, then steer clear.

Q. I've tried saying "no" to my friends, but I keep getting into trouble. What should I do?

A. Swimming against the current requires a lot of strength. It is always easier to just go with the flow. For this reason, it is important that your closest friends flow the right direction. You must surround yourself with the right kind of friends—friends who challenge you to daily live your life for Christ (adapted from *Peer Pressure*, p. 57).

As much as you will hate it, you should pull out of the group. You cannot claim to follow Christ and continue to compromise.

First Peter 2:12 says, "Keep your behavior excellent among the Gentiles, so that in the thing in which they slander you as evildoers, they may on account of your good deeds, as they observe them, glorify God in the day of visitation."

If you keep your behavior excellent, your friends may one day glorify God. If you compromise, your friends will never see any difference between your life and theirs. If they don't, what motivation will they have to become followers of Christ themselves?

Q. *How can I keep from compromising?*

A. In order not to compromise, you must become a man or woman of convictions. A conviction is a standard that you have committed yourself to keeping, regardless of what it costs you. For example, you might have a conviction that says, "Because my body is the temple of God, I will never take any illicit drugs."

Once you know what your convictions are, you will want to write them down. Writing them down helps you to remember them. It leaves less room for compromise because you know your standard and you know what action to take. You will be more motivated to follow your convictions, because it can remind you when you are in a tempting situation (adapted from *Peer Pressure*, pp. 19, 20).

As you write them, follow these guidelines.

- Use first person.
- Make them action-oriented.
- Make them specific.
- Base them on Scripture.
- Be realistic.

Live by your convictions. Don't let peer pressure persuade you otherwise. Don't compromise, regardless of the cost.

Q. *I have so many bad habits. Where does the power to say "no" come from?*

A. It takes more than just a New Year's resolution to break a bad habit. Practically it helps to plan ahead by thinking through in advance how you will respond when temptation hits again. Second, find someone to hold you accountable. Have them ask you daily or weekly, whichever is best, how the habit is doing. Third, replace the old negative habit with a new positive one.

But these practical steps will only be of little help if you decide to break old habits through will power alone. Real power comes from the Holy Spirit.

Check out the following bad habits. You find them listed in Galatians 5:19–21. "Now the deeds of the flesh are evident, which are: immorality, impurity, sensuality, idolatry, sorcery, enmities, strife, jealousy, outbursts of anger, disputes, dissensions, factions, envying, drunkenness, carousing, and things like these, of which I forewarn you just as I have forewarned you that those who practice such things shall not inherit the kingdom of God." The Bible says your bad habits originate in your flesh—that part of you that just doesn't want to cooperate, no matter how much you coax it.

To overcome these tendencies, you need the Spirit's power. Galatians 5:16 says, "But I say, walk by the Spirit, and you will not carry out the desire of the flesh." You walk by the Sprit when you obey what Christ has shown you to do and trust Him to enable you to do it.

Obviously, what we're talking about doesn't apply to the unbeliever. It only applies to Christians. Accept the dynamics of the Holy Spirit's power to change your life. Don't exclude anything. He can help you control your thoughts, your feelings, even the desire for sex, alcohol or drugs. Ask Him to do it. Then let Him!

Q. *What do I do if I blow it and give in to peer pressure again?*

A. Suppose you have taken a stand for Christ, pulled away from some of your negative friendships, and have lived for Jesus in a real and dynamic way for three straight months. After a basketball game you drop in on a party. You've had a lousy day and to take the edge off you drink a cool one. One thing leads to another and boom(!) you find yourself high as a kite.

By the time you get home, you will feel rotten, not just from the beer but also from the Holy Spirit's loving conviction. The moment you realize you've blown it, confess your disobedience to God. Psalm 32:3–5 says, "When I kept silent about my sin, my body wasted away through my groaning all day long. For day and night Thy hand was heavy upon me; My vitality was drained away as with the fever heat of summer. I acknowledged my sin to Thee, and my iniquity I did not hide; I said, 'I will confess my transgressions to the Lord'; And thou didst forgive the guilt of my sin." Once you confess your sin, you can be assured everything between you and God is right. But, in some respects, that's the easy part.

The tough part is Monday morning at school. Your behavior will give the guys at school an occasion to laugh about Christ and His followers. As soon as you get to school you must find as many of your friends as you can (Christian and non-Christian) and confess to them that what you did was wrong. Tell them you're sorry for it and ask them to forgive you.

This may be one of the hardest things you have ever done in your entire life. But it may be one of the most powerful sermons your friends will have ever heard, too. When they see a Christian blow it and admit it, they will realize that Jesus really does have control of his or her life.

Q. Wherever I am, I feel like all I ever do is just go along with the crowd. What does it take to change?

A. Romans 12:2 says, "And do not be conformed to this world, but be transformed by the renewing of your mind, that you may prove what the will of God is, that which is good and acceptable and perfect."

According to this verse, there are two groups of people: those who are becoming like the people of the world, and those who are being transformed into Christ's likeness.

To be different you must be renewed in your mind. The mind is the battlefield. If you lose the war there, you will lose it in your actions.

For example, if you are always thinking lustful thoughts, it will be all too easy to give in to the least little pressure to mess around physically, look at pornography or anything else associated with sex.

If you want to change, begin today to spend at least a few minutes every day reading, studying or memorizing God's Word. Don't just read your Bible and then forget about what you read. Think about how the verses specifically apply to your life.

Remember:

Information	+	Meditation	=	Transformation
(The Bible)		(Applying it to your life)		(A New You)

If you've never spent much time reading your Bible before, 1 John is a great place to start. Begin today and watch God's Word change your life.

First Peter 2:2 says, "Like newborn babes, long for the pure milk of the word, that by it you may grow in respect to salvation."

Q. I want to be used by God on my campus. What does it take?

A. In the country of England during the eighteenth century, the king was interviewing chariot drivers. He would ask each chariot driver the following question, "If you were driving me on a winding mountain road, how close could you come to the edge of the road without going over?" The first driver responded, "I'm so good, I could drive within 18 inches of the edge." The second driver responded, "I could drive within 6 inches of the edge." The third driver responded, "I would drive as far away from the edge as possible." The king chose the third driver. That driver was more interested in the king's welfare than in showing how great he could drive.

Many students have this attitude: "I want to see how close to the edge I can get without getting in trouble." If you want to be used by the King, have the attitude of the third servant, "To honor my King, I will see how far away from the edge I can stay."

Q. What can I do to make a difference in the lives of my friends?

A. Peer pressure exists in two forms. It can be either positive or negative.

If you want to make a difference, you must do more than resist negative peer pressure. You must exert positive peer pressure. Be an influence for Christ with your friends at school. If they don't know Christ, influence them toward becoming Christians. If they do know Christ as their personal Lord and Savior, influence them to walk closer to God and be more committed to the Lordship of Christ.

Everywhere you go, exert positive peer pressure. Try to get every person who comes within your sphere of influence to take at least one step closer to Jesus.

It only takes one person who will stand up for Jesus Christ to start a spiritual awakening on his campus. By the grace of God you could be that person.

Dare to be different. Take your stand for Jesus Christ . . . even if it means standing alone.

4 Friends.

Q. *Why do I feel so lonely, even when I'm with a lot of people?*

A. There is a tremendous difference between being alone and feeling lonely. Being alone simply means to be by yourself. When you are by yourself, you may or may not feel lonely.

A lonely person feels that way all the time, regardless of how many people surround him. It doesn't matter if you are the only person at home on Friday or walking down the hallway to your next class at school, surrounded by people. You cannot escape it.

Loneliness is that feeling you have when you must sit by yourself on the bus or at the school cafeteria. You feel as if nobody likes you, cares about you or understands you. You feel ignored, that no one will ever pay any attention to you. You feel that if you died tomorrow, nobody would even notice. Loneliness is that sad emptiness you feel deep inside.

You feel that way because you have a God-given need that perhaps is not being met. Within each of us is a desire to be loved and accepted. Until you feel that way, you will probably go on feeling lonely.

Q. *How do I get out of my loneliness?*

A. Students often respond in two ways to loneliness. Both of them are wrong. One takes the approach of, "I'm lonely because nobody loves me. Nobody loves me because I'm not lovable. I'm not lovable because I'm a worm. People step on worms, so I will never reach out to people." The worm approach doesn't do anything but aggravate your problem.

The other approach says, "I'm lonely because nobody loves me. Nobody loves me because I'm not trying hard enough. I'm going to do whatever it takes to get people's attention. Even if I make a fool of myself or compromise my standards." The make-a-fool-of-yourself approach rarely succeeds at accomplishing anything but making a fool of yourself and doing things that you tearfully regret later.

A better approach to getting out of loneliness begins with your relationship with Jesus Christ. He wants to meet the deepest needs of your life. So the first step you take moves you in the direction of strengthening your friendship with Jesus. Remember, Christ wants to be your closest friend. John 15:13 says, "Greater love has no one than this, that one lay down his life for his friends." Christ laid down His life for you. You are His Friend.

After taking this first step, you must crawl out of any worm outfits you have wiggled into. Just because you have felt lonely doesn't mean you aren't special, valuable or important. You are all three.

As a third step, you must make friends with others. And make your friendships wisely. We need other people. Otherwise God's Word wouldn't put so much emphasis in the Bible on us loving one another. First John 3:16 says, "We know love by this, that He laid down His life for us; and we ought to lay down our lives for the brethren."

Last, be patient. Making friends doesn't always happen overnight. But if you persist, you will experience the marvelous rewards that great friendships bring.

Q. *I hate being alone, like on the weekends or during summer break. Is there anything I can do about it?*

A. Being alone is not necessarily bad. If you use your time wisely, it can even be a valuable experience. The tendency is just to sit around the house, bored with nothing to do. Sure, every so often you will find diversions like playing Nintendo for fifteen solid hours, or eating six packages of chocolate chip cookies as you listen to every single one of your albums, twice, or irritating your brother or sister for awhile. But for the most part you just sit around waiting for the weekend to get over.

Have you ever considered what you might accomplish in the course of a year if you devoted just a few hours a week to something? Have you dreamed about becoming a black belt in karate, learning how to play the piano or becoming an expert in identifying and classifying fruit flies? Over the course of a school year you can accomplish major goals by trading just a couple hours of your time each week. Look at it this way. The year will march by regardless. How rewarding to have accomplished something that will benefit you for a lifetime.

Q. *I know a lot of people, but I don't feel like I have a lot of friends. What really is a friend?*

A. Some people would describe a friend as anyone that they know. Others would say only those with whom they share secret thoughts and intimate feelings are their friends. Big difference, isn't there? That's because people don't realize that there are different levels of friendships.

The first level we will call *casual* friends. This level includes the girl who has a locker beside yours, many of the students in your class, and more than likely your teachers. (You wouldn't call them your enemies, would you? Maybe you better not answer that.) Most anyone you have contact with and speak to would qualify as a casual friend.

The second level of friendship is your *close* friends. Your close friends include the people you eat with together at lunch, the ones you choose to sit by in class and the ones you go out with on the weekend.

The third and much deeper level of friendship is your *committed* friends. Where you would have lots of casual friends, several close friends, normally you have just a few committed friends. These are the friends with whom you share who you really are on the inside. They are the ones you trust and feel safe telling your secrets, hurts and joys.

So you can know lots of people, or rather have lots of casual friendships, but feel lonely because you don't have any committed friendships. It is on that third and deepest level where your needs for love and acceptance are met. It is your committed friends who take away your loneliness.

Q. Why do I need friends?

A. That's a question you may ask after your best buddies go blabbing all over school which guy you secretly love! You thought friends were supposed to take loneliness away, not cause it. At times it seems that the only useful thing friends are good for is to serve as doormats after you squash them over the head with your algebra book.

But friends are important. They do more than embarrass you and keep you from being lonely. Friends serve as comforters, counselors and challengers. When you hurt, your friend is there. They may not know what to say. They don't need to. Their just being there suffices. When you have to make a decision, you need a friend. Often their advice will do more harm than good, but just having them around gives you confidence that everything will work out. And when you need to change, if you have a friend, you will have someone to challenge you to do something about it. Friends can get you out of a bad mood or keep you from thinking you're the hottest looking guy since Elvis.

Friends affect you far more than you'll ever realize. That's why it is important that you choose your closest friends very wisely.

Q. My parents are always getting on me about my friends. They say that they aren't the kind of people they want me hanging around. What do they want me to do, be friends with Mr. Rogers?

A. Your parents probably sense something in these people's lives that is headed for trouble. And the thing that gripes every teenager is that parents more often than not, are usually right. Now they probably couldn't find this in the Bible, but they sense that these guys or gals could be a negative influence on you. (The verse happens to be 1 Corinthians 15:33, "Do not be deceived: Bad company corrupts good morals.") Therefore, since close friends have so much influence, you need to be careful who you choose as your closest friends. Being smart in how you choose your friends will go a long way not only in making your parents happy but in making you the person God wants you to be.

Q. How do I know if a friend is good for me or not?

A. Right now you are a sweet, kind, obedient, thoughtful, responsible, even angelic person. But suppose you start hanging around someone who influences you to become a smart-mouth at home or apathetic at school. When things like that happen, watch out. "Friends" like this aren't good for you regardless of how much fun you have together. They have a negative influence on you and you do not need to be that close to them.

Now it doesn't mean you can't be friends with a rowdy person or with someone who tends to get in trouble all the time. As long as you are a positive influence on such people, you can be friends with the wicked witch herself. But when someone influences you negatively, the Bible says you must back off.

Second Timothy 3:2–5 says: "For men will be lovers of self, lovers of money, boastful, arrogant, revilers, disobedient to parents, ungrateful, unholy, unloving, irreconcilable, malicious gossips, without self-control, brutal, haters of good, treacherous, reckless, conceited, lovers of pleasure rather than lovers of God; holding to a form of godliness, although they have denied its power; and avoid such men as these."

Take an honest evaluation of your friendships. If you decide that a friend is influencing you negatively you need to back off and become casual friends.

Q. *Why do I tend to attract friends who get in trouble all the time?*

A. To attract positive influence you must become a positive influencer yourself. If you aren't, you need to ask God to change you, from the inside out. Commit your life fresh and anew to following Jesus Christ and watch how it changes the kind of friends you attract.

Q. *How can I back off from a friendship that's not good for me?*

A. Backing off from a friendship is never easy—even if the friend has been a negative influence on you.

If you back off a friendship with someone, you will want to explain why. Here's what you might want to say, "You know, Delilah, I've renewed my commitment to Jesus Christ and I don't want to disappoint Him any more by doing the things I've been doing lately. If you want to do those things without me, that's up to you, but I don't want to join you anymore. If you would like to get closer to the Lord with me that would be great! What do you think?"

This is just a suggestion. Put it in your own words. Just keep in mind these pointers:

- Identify yourself with Christ.
- Display humility, not a holier-than-thou attitude.
- Be gentle in your conversation, yet firm in your decision.
- Invite your friend to join you in getting closer to Christ. If he or she does not, they left you, not you them.

Remember, it will be tough to back off, especially right afterward because of the pain of your new loneliness. But continuing the friendship would be tougher, especially in the long run, because of the friend's negative influence (adapted from *Friendships: Making the Best of Them*, p. 29).

Q. *I've just become a Christian but none of my old friends have accepted Christ. Should I still be friends with them?*

A. Yes, most definitely, because you are strategically placed to win them to Christ. But keep in mind two important principles. First, relationships have a major influence on all of us. Therefore, it is very important that you make close friendships with some Christians as quickly as possible. Your Christian friends can be a source of much strength and encouragement while you are still a "new" Christian.

On the other hand, your non-Christian friendships are just as important, but for different reasons. One reason is that you are the best person to win your old friends to Christ. But secondly, you should continue being friends with them because if you rejected them they could blame Christ for the hurt they might experience. Then whenever anyone tells them about becoming a Christian, their response could be, "Yeah sure, and reject all my friends? *No way!*"

An exception to this rule would be if they become a negative influence on you. When that happens you should distance yourself enough to play it safe. When you do back off, always give them the option of coming closer to Christ. This way, if there is rejection, it is they rejecting you, not the other way around.

Q. I have been a Christian for a while but recently I have started spending time with some non-Christians in order to win them to Christ. I'm beginning to wonder if it's worth it now. My friends at church are spreading rumors that I'm doing the same things my non-Christian friends are doing. What can I do to stop all the gossip?

A. You have just stepped on ground where few dare to tread. Christians who spend time with non-Christians usually catch it at both ends. The non-Christians make fun of you because you won't get involved, and your Christian friends gossip about you because they think you do.

But take heart. You're in great company. That was the same ground Jesus Himself chose to stand on when He walked the world. Matthew 11:19 says Christ was "a friend of tax-gatherers and sinners." And because He was, He was the subject of gossip too. Notice His response in Mark 2:16, 17, ". . . and when the scribes of the Pharisees saw that He was eating with the sinners and tax-gatherers, they began saying to His disciples, 'Why is He eating and drinking with tax-gatherers and sinners?' And hearing this, Jesus said to them, 'It is not those who are healthy who need a physician, but those who are sick; I did not come to call the righteous, but sinners.'" The best way to stop the gossip is to win one of the non-Christians to Christ. When you do, the new believer will set the record straight.

In the meantime, don't stop reaching out to your non-Christian friends. But don't get mad at your

Christian friends either. Just press on and do what Jesus did—love them both.

Q. I've just changed schools. What's the quickest way to make friends?

A. You could start by giving away money. But a better approach begins with being yourself. From the very beginning be real. Otherwise you have to go to school every day pretending to be somebody you aren't. Get involved. But remember relationships start quicker in small groups than in large ones.

Be open. Be willing to have a relationship with people different from you. Preconceived ideas of how a person ought to look or act will keep you from some super friendships.

Smile. Happy people attract others. If you always look like your cat was just run over, you can bet people will avoid you. They think what ails you might be contagious.

Talk to people. Remember: Every person you don't speak to can't become your friend. But every person you do speak to has the potential of becoming a friend.

Ask questions. Learn to carry on a conversation. Communication is basic to relationships.

Express interest. Even if you meet the most boring person in the entire world, show an interest in him. Look him in the eyes while you talk. Give him your full attention when you listen. Ask more questions about what he says. You may find that he is not as boring as you thought.

Communicate excitement. When talking, avoid being a bore yourself. If you find your friends falling asleep in front of you as you expound upon the fundamental principles of applied thermodynamics and kinetics with respect to the science of theoretical physical chemistry, you might consider changing topics regardless of how interesting it is to you. If you find every person you meet yawning when they are with you, try creating some excitement by learning new topics or hobbies. These will expose you to new skills, knowledge and experiences which in turn will make you a more interesting person.

Finally, create opportunities. There are many ways to develop friendships. Be creative: Invite a group over to your house for a get-together; send Christmas cards or birthday cards to people in your class; invite friends from school to one of your church activities.

Don't give up. You may suffer embarrassment, perhaps even face rejection, but don't let anything keep you from reaching out (adapted from *Love: Making It Last,* pp. 77–79).

Q. *People don't like me. Will I ever have any friends?*

A. More than likely, it isn't that people don't like you but probably more that people don't know you. To have friends, you have to open up and let people inside you. But then again, people actually may not like you. If that's the case, ask yourself why. You may need to change some undesirable habit or characteristic you have developed. Nobody likes being around people who are stuck up. Neither do people like to hang around someone who can't keep a confidence or who constantly criticizes. Once you determine what the habit is, ask God for the strength to change it.

If people don't like you because of your stand for

Christ, consider that an honor. First Peter 4:14–16 says, "If you are reviled for the name of Christ, you are blessed, because the Spirit of glory and of God rests upon you. By no means let any of you suffer as a murderer, or thief, or evildoer, or a troublesome meddler; but if anyone suffers as a Christian, let him not feel ashamed, but in that name let him glorify God."

Q. I'm terrible at talking to people. Will that keep me from making friends?

A. Being terrible at carrying on a conversation might not keep you from having friends, but it won't help you much either. How close could you get to someone whose entire vocabulary consisted of "I don't know"? Or "It doesn't matter to me"? And, "What do you think?"

The key to starting a great conversation and keeping it going is to ask questions. If you know how to ask questions, you don't need to do much talking. You just need to know how to listen (which is often even harder to do than to talk).

Look over these questions and pick out six or seven you really like. Memorize them and practice using them tomorrow at school. The first letters in each category form the acrostic "FRIENDSHIP."

Faith
- How did you become a Christian? When?
- Who in the Bible do you like the most? Why?

Reason
- What goals do you have?
- What is your purpose in life?

Involvements
- What extracurricular activities are you involved in?
- What do you do at your job?

Experiences
- What is Christmas like at your house?
- How have you spent your summers?

Needs
- How can I help you?
- What can I do for you?

Dreams
- Would you like to be a millionaire? Why or why not?
- What kind of impact would you like to have on the world?

School
- Which is your favorite class? Least favorite? Why?
- Do you think you will use what you are learning?

Home
- What do you like best about your parents?
- What is it like being the oldest? Youngest? Only child?

Interests
- What hobbies do you have?
- Who is your favorite music group? Why?

Prayer Requests
- How can I pray for you?
- What do you pray for yourself?

(Adapted from *Friendships:*
Making the Best of Them, p. 16.)

Q. *I've waited for someone to reach out to me to be their friend. Nothing's happened. I now feel like it's my responsibility to initiate, but I'm scared. Why?*

A. One of the biggest hindrances to building a relationship is insecurity which often expresses itself like this:

- What if he doesn't like me?
- What if I say the wrong thing?
- What if she laughs at me?
- What if I do something dumb?
- What if something goes wrong?

These negative thoughts keep you from going any deeper into a friendship. To break loose from this paralysis, you must meet your fears head on. Step out in positive faith. Every time you catch yourself dwelling on a negative fear question, change it to a positive faith statement. For example:

- I know he will like me.
- I am confident I will say the right thing.
- She will accept me.
- I will do something intelligent.
- Everything will be fine.

Generally your fears are exaggerated. They have a habit of getting out of proportion and making you pessimistic. Don't let them hold you back. Move out and make a quality friend (adapted from *Love: Making It Last*, pp. 76, 77).

Q. *Is there such a thing as best friends? If so can you have more than one?*

A. Remember the three levels of friendships? They were casual, close and committed. Normally when you speak of a best friend, you speak of a committed friend.

But what does a committed friend look like? The best way to describe a best friend is to take a look at two very committed friends in the Bible, David and Jonathan. The story of their friendship is found in I Samuel 18–20. Read it. When you finish you discover the following:

- A best friend is someone who . . .
- Loves you even when you are unlovable (20:17).
- Speaks positively about you when others don't (19:4).
- Listens to your problems (20:1, 2).
- Does things for you, regardless of the inconvenience (20:4).
- Protects you from the bad guys (20:19).
- Hurts when you hurt (20:34).
- Understands your deepest feelings (20:41).
- Is committed to you (20:42).

(Adapted from *Friendships:
Making the Best of Them*, p. 18.)

Ideally you could have hundreds of best friends. But practically speaking, a person can only be this kind of friend to just a few people.

Q. How can I become best friends with someone?

A. Most of us would probably like to have more friends. It takes skill to develop and keep friends. Apply these skills and it will help you to form friendships that will last a lifetime. Here are some keys to developing your friendship skills:

Feel good about yourself. Develop a good self-image. If you don't like yourself, it will be difficult to like others properly.

Accept people for who they are. All of us have uniquenesses—that's what makes us unique! Avoid judging or condemning others even if they're sometimes offensive. Overlook their faults. "If you accept me for who I am, I am more apt to change than if you demand that I change."

Be positive and encouraging. Most people live in environments of constant criticism. Learn to build people up. You will be a breath of fresh air.

Practice confidentiality. Stop immediately if you ever find yourself saying, "So-and-so told me not to tell anyone, but I know she won't mind if I tell you."

Be a good listener by: communicating good body language; requesting more information; reflecting on what is being said; repeating statements with feeling; and remaining silent when another is telling a story.

Finally, *be patient.* It takes lots of time to build close and committed friendships.

Q. I get a close friend and then do something that messes up the friendship. What am I doing wrong?

A. The following things kill friendship. If you want to make and keep friends, avoid them:

Jealousy. Why not celebrate your friend's achievements and good fortunes, rather than envying them?

Gossip. Teeter-totter principle: You bring yourself up, by tearing others down.

Disloyalty. You say you are his/her friend. But under certain circumstances you turn on him/her.

Competition. Friendship is not a race you both run as competitors. Instead, we cheer each other on.

Negativism. True, misery loves miserable company. Up to a point. Beyond that, your complaining will make your friends scarce.

Comparison. If you compare yourself to others, you're asking for friendship hassles.

Selfishness. Friendship is built on the idea that you have time to serve others' interests, not solely your own. If you turn everything inward, you will turn others away. (*Campus Life Magazine,* 1985, p. 20).

Identify which of these friendship killers you have and begin ridding yourself of them.

Q. *Is there such a thing as friends forever?*

A. Yes and no. You will meet some people who you remain close to for the rest of your life. But, unfortunately, that is not always the case. Friendships change and for many different reasons.

As you grow and mature as a person, you will sometimes find that you and one of your close friends will no longer enjoy doing the same thing and will drift apart. Friendships often change soon after graduation. If you go off to different colleges you may rarely see each other again. That, and that alone, is the only sad part about breaking out of Prison High.

Some friends move, just as you were getting close. Others get married and start a whole new life.

Regardless of the reason, you wake up one day and realize things aren't the same anymore. It's always sad when that happens, but be positive about it. There will be new friends and you can enjoy the memories your old friends left behind.

Q. How can I convince someone of the opposite sex that I really do want to be just good friends?

A. Every week at school there is at least one JGF (just good friends) game going on. They remind you of soap operas. Monday—guy meets gal and checks her out while girl meets guy and checks him out. Tuesday—the guy's chemistry (or the gal's, depending on which channel you're watching) says, "Great potential for a date!" The gal's chemistry says, "Great potential for the zoo. Somebody better lock the animal up in a hurry." Wednesday—guy stalks girl down hallway. Gal hides in bathroom for three hours in fear that he's waiting outside. Thursday—guy is convinced she loves him. Gal is convinced he's mentally deranged. Friday—guy finally gets the message she's not interested. Gal breathes sigh of relief, looks forward to making a new friendship. Guy feels humiliated and doesn't show his face around gal for the rest of the school year. And the soap continues the next week but with different characters.

Another potential friendship down the tubes because someone of the opposite sex wanted to be more than "just good friends."

To play the JGF game you must know the rules of

the game. Rule number one: Avoid being a flirt. Sometimes it is easier to go through your day without blinking. But flirting makes the opposite sex act stranger and weirder than they already are.

Rule number two: Realize that even when you don't flirt, some guy or gal is going to go ape over you.

Rule number three: When someone does go wild over you, be patient and understanding with them. Don't lead them on, but don't run from them either. Keep in mind that in a few days they will realize that you are serious about being JGF. When they finally get that in their head they can relax and enjoy the friendship.

Q. Why do my best friends and I fight over the least little things?

A. Friendships go through stages. The first stage is the I'm-getting-to-know-you stage. During this stage you learn about each other. Then you move to the I'm-getting-to-know-you-better stage. This stage holds the potential for the most fun. The third stage is I'm-getting-to-know-you-all-too-well stage. During this stage you've come to know each other so well you say the same things at the same time. But you have also gotten to know each other's negative traits, and they bug the daylights out of you.

If you haven't experienced any conflict with your best friend yet, either (a) your best friend is an imaginary friend, or (b) you really don't know each other well enough yet. Because when you get to know someone really well, conflict is inevitable. No two people are exactly the same. They have different backgrounds, different perspectives and different desires. Sooner or later you will have a disagreement. But as you learn how to handle your conflicts your friendships can grow.

Q. If my friend and I have a disagreement, what's the right way to handle it?

A. When you have a disagreement, you have a choice. You can either resolve the conflict or dissolve the relationship. Here are some guidelines for resolving the conflict and keeping the fight fair:

Desire openness. In a fair fight, the attitude of "I'm always right" is against the rules.

Choose the right timing. Arguments can break out at awkward times. To fight by the rules, wait until both of you can give the time and attention necessary to talk things out.

Select the right words. Think before you speak. To know the right words to say, you'll first have to listen to your friend when she speaks. Determine if your words will help or hinder in working out the problem.

Guard your tone of voice. You can say the right words the wrong way. If you project sarcasm or criticism in your voice, your friend will pick it up.

Look at the other person's point of view. While your friend talks, listen carefully to understand where they are coming from. In viewing the conflict, put yourself in their place. When you do this, think of how they feel instead of how you feel or why you think they were wrong.

Identify the problem. Discover the main issue that started the fight. It may be more than meets the eye. For example, they may have become upset because you said the wrong thing when actually they were already upset because the night before you spent time with another friend.

Determine the solution. Once you identify the problem, decide on a solution. Make the solution practical and realistic. Don't give up until you have worked things out satisfactorily. Talk about how to keep this conflict from happening again (adapted from *Friends: Making the Best of Them*, pp. 45–48).

Q. Why is it so difficult to get things back together with my friend after we've had a fight?

A. When a disagreement with a friend is not handled properly, we react in ways that really hurt our friendship. Do any of these sound familiar?

Silent treatment. People who use this tactic become very quiet when things don't go their way. When asked, "What's wrong?" their standard reply is, "Nothing." Generally they assume the fighting stance of arms crossed, teeth clenched and eyes staring straight ahead.

Blow 'em away. Explosive describes this style. When upset these people start yelling and screaming. If you are unfortunate enough to catch one of them in action, you will easily recognize them. Such people break objects, stomp around, wave their arms wildly and scream bloody murder. If you think you have spotted one, but still are not sure, check out his or her opponents for further proof. The opponent's hair looks like he just stepped out of a convertible.

Cry 'til I die. When conflict arises, some people begin to cry. They cry. And cry. And cry. The other person feels sorry for this poor puddle of tears and gives in out of pity. This approach is successful if a person's goal is to get his or her way. These warriors can be recognized by their red puffy eyes, somber face and the mutilated tissues they carry around.

Smart-mouth. Sarcasm characterizes some people when they are on the warpath. Their comments can be biting and stinging. You will notice them by the cocky position of their heads and the turned-up noses. Their opponents have darts sticking out of their bodies.

Go for the throat. Some have never returned after crossing a person who fights with this ferocious and ruthless style. When upset, this person goes for the kill. He has no mercy. He lets you know every fault. He tells you everything you have ever done wrong. He tears you down and then rips you up. You recognize this fighter by the blood in his eyes and the smoke coming out of his nostrils.

Turn and run. Instead of fighting, some people run, avoiding conflict at all costs. To them, fighting is frightening. At the first sign of trouble they head for the hills. If they can't run physically, they withdraw into a shell. You will recognize them by their absence (adapted from *Love: Making It Last,* pp. 88, 89).

Responding in any of the above ways puts up a big wall that has to be handled before your friendship can return to normal.

A second wall is inside you. It's called Pride! We think, *No way am I going to try and get things right. They started it. They are going to have to come crawling back to me.* Matthew 5:23–24 says, "If therefore you are presenting your offering at the altar, and there remember that your brother has something against you, leave your offering there before the altar, and go your way; first be reconciled to your brother, and then come and present your offering."

To get the relationship right, you (that's spelled Y-O-U) must first humble yourself and go to your friend and apologize for acting like a jerk. Friendships are too precious to stay mad. Make the first move and make it quickly.

Q. Is any personality better than another? I feel like mine is terrible.

A. Hippocrates, a man who lived centuries before the birth of Christ, noticed the similarities in certain people. As a result he divided people into four groups according to their personalities: sanguine, choleric, melancholy and phlegmatic. These terms and groups are still helpful to classify general personality types.

Sanguine	*Choleric*	*Melancholy*	*Phlegmatic*
Playful	Persuasive	Persistent	Peaceful
Sociable	Strong-willed	Self-sacrificing	Submissive
Optimistic	Outspoken	Orderly	Obliging
Funny	Forceful	Faithful	Friendly
Lively	Leader	Loyal	Listener
Undisciplined	Unsympathetic	Unforgiving	Unenthusiastic
Forgetful	Frank	Fussy	Fearful
Interrupts	Impatient	Insecure	Indecisive
Unpredictable	Unaffectionate	Unpopular	Uninvolved
Haphazard	Headstrong	Hard-to-please	Hesitant

Each personality type offers its own strengths, but it also has its weaknesses. For example, a sanguine talks easily with others (strength), but at times these people can talk you to death (weakness). A choleric loves getting jobs done (strength), but tends to be insensitive to the needs of others (weakness). A melancholy is very thorough (strength), but can become too picky (weakness). A phlegmatic rarely gets uptight (strength), but can become lazy (weakness) (adapted from *Friends: Making the Best of Them,* pp. 40–42).

Q. *Should I try to change my personality?*

A. You were basically born with a certain personality but that doesn't mean you can't modify or strengthen it. We're all expected to change and adapt. It's a cop-out to blame fights with your friends on your personality by saying, "That's just the way I am."

Perhaps you and a friend have found yourself in that type of situation before. If so, you need to work on diminishing your weaknesses and developing your strengths.

Q. *Is it wrong to be a part of a clique?*

A. Everybody is a part of one clique or another at school. You just can't help it. You may be a part of a really big clique like the football players' clique, or a really small clique like yours and your best friend's clique. Your clique may be popular like the cheerleaders' clique or unpopular like the chess club's clique.

Being a part of a clique is not wrong, unless that clique is exclusive. That is, your group accepts some people and rejects others.

Q. *What will people think of me if I'm friends with someone who isn't socially accepted?*

A. At one time or another we all have had somebody who was "different" want to be our friend. But fear that our reputation would suffer has kept us from reaching out to this "untouchable."

The main question is not what will your friends think of you if you do reach out, but what will God think of you if you don't? First John 3:18 says, "Little children, let us not love with word or with tongue, but in deed and truth."

The next time someone different looks to you for friendship, reach out to him. You may learn something special through this person. So don't look at people in terms of whether they are socially acceptable or not. See them as people God Himself has placed in your life. When you do, He will take care of your reputation.

Q. What do I do if I'm a part of a clique that's excluding people?

A. Your first responsibility is to look to yourself. If you have done the same thing, you need to see it for what it is, rejecting people. Your second responsibility is to the clique. Challenge your friends to let others be a part of "the group." If the group refuses to change and continues to reject people, then you should let the group know that you are going to be different and invite people to join the group in the cafeteria or in some of your activities. If they reject your new friend by ignoring him or her, then they are in essence rejecting you.

Q. I feel it's really important to have my friends respect me. How should I handle it when they laugh at me?

A. You beg your mom not to send you to school. You fake sick. You play dead. Nothing works. You arrive at school just before the bell rings.

You walk into class trying to turn invisible. (You're a little on the anorexic side, but invisible you ain't.) As you come down the aisle you notice your boyfriends' eyes bug out. Then you hear the worst sound you could ever hear in your entire life at this point—laughter.

Where'd you get your hair done? Acme Electric Company? HA HA HA HA HA HA! What color is that anyway? Fluorescent green? HA HA HA HA HA HA! What on earth built that nest on your head? HA HA HA HA!

You sit there, doing everything you know to hold back the tears. Fluorescent green may look good on Patti Punker, but not you. You wanted your hair to look like it had really bleached out in the sun during the summer, so you scraped together some money and risked letting the hairdresser bleach it a little—just a little, you told her.

She didn't just goof up your hair; she ruined your life.

It's not fun when your friends laugh at your fluorescent green hair, but it is understandable. The next time friends laugh at you, if at all possible, laugh with them. Don't take yourself too seriously. But when the laughter hurts, go to a friend and share your hurt. Talking it out can help you see it in perspective.

Q. What should I do if one of my friends invites everyone else over but leaves me out?

A. You make your way through the maze of chairs and tables in the school cafeteria. You head toward "your" table, where you always sit with your friends. Trying not to spill your food (at least that's what the cafeteria staff calls it) you expertly balance your tray in one hand and pull your chair out with the other. You sit down just in time to hear, "So we'll meet at 6:30 tonight."

"Where are we going?" you ask, completely unprepared for the deathly silence that follows (adapted from *Friends: Making the Best of Them*, pp. 51, 52).

Whenever you get left out, first go to Jesus. Be honest with Him about your emotions. Then try to understand why you were left out. Was it an oversight, was it circumstances or did they really not want you around? Third, forgive the person. Don't let bitterness and anger rip you off. Break out of the rut. Don't stay home throwing a pity-party. Get out and do something to take your mind off your situation. Finally, when you get to school, guard your tongue. Don't make nasty comments behind your friends' backs. And when you see them face to face, don't give in to those feelings of insecurity. Go up to them and ask them how the get-together went—not sarcastically but out of a genuine concern. Give them a second chance at being your friend.

Q. Do friends exist who will never hurt me? One who will love and accept me just like I am?

A. Unfortunately, people are not perfect. Because they are human, sooner or later they will disappoint you.

However, there is someone who will never disappoint you. There is someone who can meet all your needs. Jesus Christ is the ideal friend. He knows you inside and out, yet loves you at all times.

He will go through the problems of life with you and never leave you. Jesus Christ will encourage you, counsel you and challenge you to reach your potential.

So your need for friendship should be met first and foremost by developing your personal relationship with Jesus Christ. When you do not allow Him to become your best friend, you will always be lonely regardless of how many "friends" you may have. But if He is your friend, you may be alone but you will never by lonely. When you feel lonely, spend time with Him (adapted from *Love: Making It Last*, p. 75).

Q. How can I grow in my friendship with Christ?

A. You begin a relationship with Christ by inviting Him to come into you life. You grow in that relationship by spending time with Jesus every day. Spend part of that time talking to Him in prayer. Spend the other part of that time by listening to Him as you read your Bible. Set ten minutes aside today to do both and watch your friendship with Christ take off.

Q. What do I do when my friend starts out with, "Promise not to tell . . . "?

A. This is a touchy subject. So let us give the worst case scenario. Suppose you say, "Okay, I won't tell anybody." And then they say something like: "I'm gay," "I'm doing drugs," "I'm pregnant," "I'm going to commit suicide," "I'm going to get an abortion," "I'm being abused by my father."

So here you are, a month later in the emergency room at the hospital, looking your friend's mother in the eyes and she asks, "If you knew, then why didn't you tell me?"

When you give your word, you must honor it. But it's not wise to commit yourself to secrecy before you know what your friend is going to tell you.

The best approach is to answer, "You know I am committed to you and our friendship. If it's best not to tell, I won't. But I can't promise that I would never tell before I know what it is. If you feel like I shouldn't know, then don't tell me. That's okay with me."

Your friend might think you're weird. But not if one day it kept him or her out of some serious trouble.

Q. What do I do when one of my friends is really suffering?

A. Often one of your friends may experience hurt whether it's from a divorce by their parents, flunking a big test or not making the team. You can help your friend, even when you don't really know what to say. Ecclesiastes 4:9, 10 says, "Two are better than one because they have a good return for their labor. For if either of them falls, the one will lift up his companion. But woe to the one who falls when there is not another to lift him up."

First, affirm his value and importance by loving him. Never assume that your friends know you love or care for them. Tell them. Show them by hugging them.

Second, give them a chance to talk if they need to ventilate their feelings. You might ask, "Do you need someone to talk to?" If they do, let them talk. You don't need to say anything. Just listen. That's the best thing you can do.

Third, grieve with them. Learn to open your heart up to the feelings of people. Although you won't understand completely, when you grieve with a friend, his grief is cut in half.

Finally, pray for and with your friend. Point them to the One who wants to take care of all their hurts.

Dating

Q. Is dating in the Bible?

A. You can't find dating mentioned in the Bible for the same reason you can't find Sunday school in the Bible. Dating, like Sunday school, was not a part of society during biblical times. Back then, most marriages were arranged by the parents. Check out Genesis 24.

Wouldn't that be a great way to go today? Just think of it! No worries about becoming an old maid. No problem about finding a date for the prom. No more pressure from your friends to go out with some loser. No more dateless Friday nights. Your biggest worry would be deciding who to double with.

Drawbacks do exist, however. That marriage partner your parents pick out for you may be the cutest kid on the block when he's a baby. But you never know if he will still suck his thumb when he reaches high school. Or they might set you up with a girl who at 6'6" is still growing and you maxed out at 5'4".

Given the alternative, you probably are glad for the present-day system of dating. After all, if your parents can't pick out the kind of clothes you like, how in the world could they pick out the kind of marriage partner you would like?

Although you can't find dating in the Bible you can find, on just about every page, scripture verses that apply to your dating relationships. As we answer the questions below, we will draw attention to many of these.

Q. I have been going out with one guy and told him I wanted to be just friends. But he got mad when I went out with another guy. What did I do wrong?

A. Some people enter dating with an attitude of "ownership." They think that you belong to them and refuse to allow you to live your own life. They act as if you are their private property and want you to fulfill their every desire.

Then there are those who approach dating with an attitude of "relationship." They put all the emphasis on being "in love." They major on the romantic and become very insecure and jealous when you go out with another person.

Philippians 2:3, 4 expresses the right attitude you should have about dating. It says, "Do nothing from selfishness or empty conceit, but with humility of mind let each of you regard one another as more important than himself; do not merely look out for your own personal interests, but also for the interests of others." The right attitude is that of "friendship." The purpose of dating is not to meet *your* needs, but the needs of the other person. It is not to grow "in love," but to grow in friendship. Some people, no matter how much you communicate this attitude, just will not understand. When that happens, be patient with them. Make every effort to remind them of the fact that they are still your friend. Hopefully, after a while, they will see your point of view.

Q. I'm fourteen years old and all my friends are dating. My parents say I can't date until I'm sixteen. I don't think that's fair. How old should I be before I can start dating?

A. Few issues cause as much conflict in the home as the question of "how old is old enough to date?" Some parents think you shouldn't date until after you're married. Students think they are born ready to date.

You might be surprised to know that it's not a physical age but a spiritual and emotional maturity that determines whether you are old enough to date. When my (Josh) two oldest children were twelve and fourteen years old, they asked me this same question. I was honest and told them, "I don't know. It depends on each of you. You're not old enough to date until you've developed the emotional and spiritual maturity to say no to sexual pressure. In other words," I said, "you're old enough to date when you show the character and maturity to put off immediate satisfaction to the future." It was interesting that both of my children agreed with me.

How can you know if you are mature enough to date? Here are some evidences:

- Your choices are not determined.
- You aren't influenced by peer pressure.
- Your self-image is not based on whether you are dating or not.
- You date for the purpose of friendship not romance.
- You have committed yourself to purity and will not compromise with sex.
- You have your parents' permission.

Even though your maturity determines whether you are ready to date, physical age does have a lot to do with it. Consider these statistics. The first column is the age girls started dating. The next column shows how many ended up having sex before graduating.

Age	Blew It
12	91%
13	56%
14	53%
15	41%
16	20%

Q. *I'm dating a guy who is five years older than I. Is there anything wrong with that?*

A. It depends on how old you are right now. If you are fifteen and dating a ten-year-old or eighteen dating a thirteen-year-old, then some questions need to be asked like, "Why are you dating someone that much younger than yourself?" Most people who date someone that much younger than themselves do so because of ego, insecurity, wanting to control the relationship or having something on their minds besides movies and popcorn.

But say you are eighty-five dating an eighty-year-old, or twenty-six dating a twenty-one-year-old. There's a big difference, not in age but in maturity, interests, perspectives.

If you are considering dating someone significantly older than yourself, you need to search for the reason why. Often a five-year age difference for a teenager is not very safe. Generally speaking, you would be wise to stick within a two-year age difference.

Q. *My dad won't let me date any of the guys who ask me out. He is too protective. Even my mom thinks so. What can I do to get him to loosen up some?*

A. First, understand where your dad is coming from. All of your life you have been his "little girl." Now some guy wants to date you and take you away from him. Just the thought of it starts his protective juices to flowing.

Dads picture the worst when their daughters begin dating. Not only do they fear that they will lose you, but they have other fears as well. One is, they fear you might get too close physically with the guy. It's not that he doesn't trust you as much as he doesn't trust the guy's hormones. He also fears that you might get your heart broken. It almost kills a daddy to see his "baby" hurt over anything. Especially if he thinks he could have protected you from the pain by not letting you date a jerk (translated—any guy who wants to date his daughter).

So understand your dad. Then communicate with him where you are in your dating standards. Let him know what qualities you look for in someone before you date them. Tell him about the stand you've taken to remain physically pure—no compromise. Talk about the alternatives to couple dating like double dating or group dating. In time your dad will likely give you more freedom.

Q. *Does it matter what kind of person I go out with?*

A. The most important aspect about dating is who you go out with—because you marry who you date. If you date a loser, you will marry a loser. If you date a winner, you will marry a winner.

But what makes a winner? It is what's on the inside that makes a person a winner. It has nothing to do with looks. This doesn't mean you have to date ugly people or that you shouldn't seek to look your best.

But if you are looking to date somebody, put the emphasis on what kind of person he or she is on the inside. Are their inner qualities consistent with yours and biblical standards? If they are, you have found a winner and someone you can go out with.

Q.   All the Christian girls in my school look like Popeye's girl (Olive Oil). Do I have to go out with someone like that?

A.   Sure, the kids at school probably put a lot of pressure on you to date only the "lookers." That's the world's system of dating. It "glorifies the kids who are already glorified by our society and puts down the kids who are already put down."

Tony Campolo puts it like this, "The system tends to get young people to put a premium on personal traits and characteristics which, in the long range of life, prove to be superficial. On the contrary, a number of things that really count are ignored. The kids who make it in the dating system are usually good-looking, but may be shallow, while many quality people who aren't so good-looking don't stand a chance" (from *A Straight Word to Kids and Parents,* p. 66).

If your motivation for going out with someone is friendship, it shouldn't matter how she looks as long as she is a winner inwardly.

Don't get hung up too much on looks because looks don't last. Let your motivation for dating be to encourage and build up people. Don't let your ego stand in the way.

Q.   I'm white and really like a black friend of mine. Is it okay to date someone of another race?

A. This question needs to be answered on three different levels. Scripturally, there doesn't seem to be anything wrong with dating or marrying someone of a different race. Colossians 3:10, 11 says, "And have put on the new self who is being renewed to a true knowledge according to the image of the One who created him—a renewal in which there is no distinction between Greek and Jew, circumcised and uncircumcised, barbarian, Scythian, slave and freeman, but Christ is all, and in all."

Culturally is where you run into problems. Take the United States, for example. In parts of the South, a black and white would be severely persecuted by people who "think" it is wrong. Actually these people are just prejudiced. They have little understanding of the unconditional love of Christ.

But take this same couple and move them out West and they would have far fewer problems. The couples out West who often have problems are whites and Hispanics who date. A different area of the country—a different form of prejudice.

So culturally you may have problems. And not just you and your date, but your children could face problems. The question then becomes not is it right or wrong, but wise or unwise to date.

Q. *What's wrong with dating non-Christians?*

A. The Bible says, "Do not be bound together with unbelievers" (2 Cor. 6:14).

This can be tough to accept, especially when the oldest Christian guy in town is only nine years old! It gets lonely not going out. The longer you wait, the more attractive non-Christians become.

The tendency is to start to make excuses like:

He understands me.
She accepts me for who I am.
I haven't gone out in a long time, and I'm lonely.
There aren't any Christians I want to date.
Non-Christians have more fun than Christians.
She's nicer than the Christian girls I know.
He's really changing. He's not at all like he was.
I'm not going to marry her.
I'll go out with him only once or twice.
My friends want me to go and I'll disappoint them if I don't.
Everyone will think I'm stuck-up.
I don't know how to say "no" when a non-Christian asks me out.
I might lead him (or her) to Christ (adapted from *Dating: Picking (and Being) a Winner*, pp. 50, 51).

Q. *What if I lead the non-Christian whom I'm dating to Christ? Won't that make it all worthwhile?*

A. But what if he doesn't accept Christ and you get married? Consider these possible consequences:

Loneliness. Because the non-Christian is dead spiritually, he cannot communicate with the spouse about many important things that mean much to a Christian.

Disappointment. The non-Christian said he would change, but didn't.

Mistrust. Because of the lies and hurt, now it is hard to trust the non-Christian spouse.

Pressure. The Christian desperately wants the spouse to change so he begins to nag and preach.

Resentment. Because of the pressure to change, the spouse gets angry and goes further in the other direction.

Guilt. Feelings of guilt result from getting into this situation. The Christian feels like he's let everyone down—himself, his family and God.

Depression. All the joy is gone. All that's left are the scars and heartaches.

Fear. The Christian realizes that he will have to start life all over with nowhere to go. That frightens him. The future seems terribly bleak.

The Next Generation. Rarely do people think beyond themselves. Children suffer tremendously because of a wrong decision to marry (adapted from *Dating: Picking (and Being) a Winner,* pp. 54, 55).

Q. *Why are girls so strange?*

A. Guys, have you ever wondered why girls giggle all the time? Or why they cry, even when they're happy? Why you can't get a girl to pay attention to you and then when she does, why you can't get her to quit paying attention to you?

If you haven't noticed by now, girls are different from guys—in more than just physical ways. They are often better tuned to their emotions than guys. That's why after dinner, they will talk more about the atmosphere of the restaurant than how many toppings you ordered on the pizza.

Girls are sometimes more romantic than guys. They appreciate and respond to the "little things" like cards, flowers, thoughtful acts or even the tone of your voice.

Rather than be frustrated by behavior or responses you don't understand, rejoice! Be glad they are different.

A gal's differences can compliment the way you were made (adapted from *Sex: Desiring the Best,* pp. 39–41).

Q. *What does it take to get a gal interested in me?*

A. If you think that good looks, a new car or lots of money gets a gal's attention, you're right! They do. But they play such a small part in it. For most girls, what impresses them the most is a guy who cares about a girl's feelings. Girls enjoy talking to guys who really listen.

That's why some of the guys you think could never get a girl can have two or three dates a weekend with really popular girls. The guy has learned the secret of being attractive to girls.

Probably the most helpful advice we can give you is to be yourself. Don't feel like you have to be someone you're not. If you have habits that are repulsive, like treating a gal like one of the guys, change your ways! But remember. Who you are is far more attractive to a girl than what you look like. Learn a girl's interests and share those interests with her. You'll be surprised how the word will travel that you are an interesting guy to go out with.

Q. *How do I ask a girl out?*

A. Once you've found a girl you would like to date, and you know her well enough, then try calling her on the phone.

After you talk for a while, you're ready to ask the question. In asking, never have the attitude: "You wouldn't want to go out with me, would you?" If you ask like that she will think you have a disease.

Nor should you have the attitude: "Of course you would like the privilege of going out with me since I am

God's gift to women. When would you like to pick me up?" Or, don't cop out by asking, "Are you doing anything Friday night?"

One of the best ways to pop the question is to ask it like this: "You know, Hermanatica, I've enjoyed talking with you. Would you like to get together Tuesday of next week at 3 P.M. to look for lost golf balls at Frank's Miniature Golf? That way we could get to know each other better."

When you ask her, always include when and what you plan to do specifically. Never just ask if she would like to go out. If she thinks you are a turkey, you have left her only two options: (1) She can go out and be miserable, or (2) she can turn you down and hurt your feelings.

Telling her the time of the date gives her a polite way of excusing herself if she doesn't want to go. If she says she is committed, it's okay to say, "Maybe we could go out another time," and see what she says. But don't fish for another date. If she wants to go out with you, she will apologize and let you know she would like for you to ask her out again. She might even offer nights when she is available. If this happens, don't waste any time in getting the date. Nail it down on the spot.

Planning the date ahead of time shows the girl you have thought this date through. This makes her feel special. Consider setting up a group date for the first date. It relaxes the pressure and often girls are more willing to go out in that situation (adapted from *Dating: Picking (and Being) a Winner*, pp. 69–70).

Q. *How can I let a guy know I'm interested in him without making a complete fool of myself?*

A. First Peter 3:3, 4 says, "And let not your adornment be merely external—braiding the hair, and wearing gold jewelry, or putting on dresses; but let it be the hidden person of the heart, with the imperishable quality of a gentle and quiet spirit, which is precious in the sight of God."

These verses give three principles. First, *look your best.* You want to emphasize your inward beauty, but don't neglect your outward beauty. If certain makeup or styles of clothing can enhance your beauty, take advantage of them without overdoing it. And be careful in your dressing to draw attention to your face, not your assets.

Second, *reflect inner beauty.* You can do this by acting out qualities such as being courteous, kind, thoughtful, appreciative, etc. Guys can respect someone they don't love, but they will never love anyone they don't respect.

Lastly, *try writing a note* with something like: "I'm glad our relationship is developing and I hope it continues." The best way to win his attention is by becoming his friend.

Q. Is it okay for a girl to ask a guy out for a date?

A. There are circumstances where it is very appropriate for a girl to ask a guy out, like a banquet that's hosted by a club or your church where you are encouraged to bring a date.

It's okay for a girl to take the initiative, especially in getting a friendship started. Some guys have difficulties initiating and a girl can help get things rolling. Asking a guy to a group meeting is a good example. But a person, whether guy or girl, needs to be careful they're not the one "pushing" the relationship. Dating needs to be a mutual understanding between both guys and girls.

Q. *Should a girl play hard to get?*

A. Dating isn't really a game to be played but if it were, here are some rules for winning:

Object of Game:

Make as many people feel special as you possibly can.

Rules of Game:

1. Let character qualities, not popularity, decide who you go out with.
2. Major on friendship. If romance follows, that's fine. But do not go looking for it.
3. You do not own the other person so always give him or her the freedom to date other people.

Helps in Playing the Game:

1. Keep your security in Christ not the relationship or what people think of you or who you're dating.
2. Treat the date as you would want someone to be treating your future spouse.
3. Major on becoming the best person inwardly you possibly can be.
4. To really grow close and be friends after you date, avoid the physical.

Q. *Is it wrong to flirt with guys?*

A. A girl can get a guy's attention and a date in two ways: 1) You can be a flirt, someone who makes insincere advances by using sexual attraction. Or, 2) you can be a friend.

Don't misunderstand. An outgoing personality is not flirting. Flirting can often give a guy the wrong impression by focusing the relationship on the physical. On the other hand an outgoing personality can express friendliness. And when your friendship attracts a guy, you start your dating relationship on a solid foundation.

A fine line exists between flirting and an outgoing friendliness. So be conscious of your motivation (adapted from *Dating: Picking (and Being) a Winner,* pp. 83, 84).

Q. Is it okay for a girl to call a guy on the phone?

A. Guys tell us they don't mind it when a girl calls them as long as they don't become a pest. If two people are good friends it doesn't matter who initiates the call. The important thing is to be sensitive to whether the other person wants to be called.

Q. What do I do if a good friend asks me out but I don't want to date him?

A. Communication is the key. Be honest and up front with your friend. Don't put it off or you will soon start to avoid him, bringing potential harm to the friendship. The purpose of dating is to grow in friendship but you don't have to date every friend.

On the other hand, why not go out with him? If you are afraid he likes you too much, communicate clearly that you don't think it's best to become romantically involved. And if you go out and you sense he has gotten romantically involved tell him it makes you feel uncomfortable. If he is unable to make it a friendship relationship, don't go out with him again.

Q. *Why do "nice" girls always get bothered by the guys they least want to go out with, just for being friendly?*

A. Guys sometimes misinterpret friendliness. They often read too much into it. It is natural for a guy who is hungry for attraction to hope that your friendliness is more than it is. The challenge is to let him know you don't want to go out with him without making him feel rejected. With some guys this may not be easy.

Q. *What's the best way to turn down a date?*

A. Turning down a date requires a balance between being gentle and firm. But regardless of how gently you say no, the guy will be hurt at least a little bit. The longer you put it off the worse it will hurt. Guys want to know early on so they won't make fools of themselves. Often an explanation as to why you turned him down will help ease the pain. If you really would like for the guy to ask you again in the future, tell him so.

Regardless of the situation, always let the guy know how much you appreciate his kind offer by thanking him for the invitation.

Q. *How should I act when I ask a girl out and she turns me down?*

A. Dating may feel like everything, but it's not. Your value and importance comes from who you are, not how often you date or who you go out with.

Continue to be the girl's friend. Don't back off from

the friendship just because she didn't want to date you. Let your security in Christ enable you to be yourself around the girl who turned you down.

Q.   I haven't been out on a date in six months. Why can't I find someone to date?

A.   There's a principle in dating that says: To date the best, you must become the best. If you want to date a prince, you must become a princess. If you want to date a princess, you must become a prince.

Avoid negative thinking while you are waiting on your prince or princess to show up. It's easy to think thoughts like: *My life is being wasted. I'm a reject. Something must be the matter with me. I will never get married. I'll be lonely the rest of my life. I'll die an old maid.*

Instead, channel your energies into growing as a person: spiritually, mentally, physically and socially. All kinds of opportunities exist for you to take advantage of. Whatever you do, don't waste the time. It's a tremendous opportunity for you to develop as a person. Get the most out of the waiting time. One day your future prince or princess will be glad you did.

Q.   What do girls want to do on dates?

A.   Girls tell us they enjoy variety. Some say they enjoy fancy places and yet find casual dates fun too. However, every girl is different. The best thing is to get to know her interests and do those things that match her interests. Girls also tell us they enjoy group dates.

A lot of girls are much more impressed with creativity then money. Creativity tells the girls the guy is thinking about them.

Q. What else can we do on a date besides see a movie and eat pizza?

A. Hundreds of different kinds of dates exist if you dare to be creative. Here's how to put together a dynamite date. First, determine what kind of date she would most enjoy. Does she get into sporting events (like a basketball game), being outdoors (like a picnic), doing crazy things (like learning to drive a stick shift), attending the performing arts (like a musical), ministering to others (like going to an orphanage to love on the kids), going out to dinner (like a French restaurant) or just the old standby, watching movies? Next, count up your money. If you are low on cash that week, there are plenty of things to do that don't cost a lot of money like walking through a mall and eating ice cream together. Try to think of something where you can maximize the talk time. Movies are the worst. Take the time to plan out every minute of the date. It makes the girl feel special to think that you are concerned enough about her that you planned out the details. Try to include other people. Group dates add a fantastic dynamic. Pick different times to go out, like going to breakfast.

Following these suggestions will add great variety to your dates. It will take a little more work, but it will be worth it. The gals will love it.

Q. Who pays for the date?

A. Generally speaking, whoever initiates pays for the date. There are exceptions, however. If it is a group date and you aren't paired off, each person usually pays for his own. Sometimes the guy will ask a girl out but ask if there is any problem going dutch. That means, everyone pays their own way.

In today's culture it can be healthy to have each pay their own way. In a very subtle sense, our society communicates that if a guy has treated a girl to a date, then he deserves something more—sex. A girl often can feel a sexual obligation after a guy has treated her to dinner and a movie. When a girl pays her own way, that eliminates some of the pressure and even reduces the dangers of date rape.

Q. What do girls think about guys praying on dates?

A. The Christian girls we talk to think it's great. But they want you to do it because you want to, not because you think it's expected. Prayer is appropriate any time. *Take the lead.*

Q. Is it okay to talk about sex on a date?

A. If the topic comes up in the conversation, it is best to state your convictions (your commitment to purity) and then move on to a different topic. Besides, other than telling each other about your commitment to purity, what else is there to say about it that will encourage each other to remain pure?

Q. Are there any advantages to group dating?

A. Group dating has many advantages. First and foremost, you can include the people who are left out in the world's system of dating. Too many people enter high school with a fairly good self-image, but by the time they graduate their sense of value, worth and significance has been devastated. They have fallen for the lie that tells them if they didn't date regularly, if they weren't popular or if no one ever fell in love with them, then they are failures.

Group dating has other advantages. Few experiences are as fun as being a part of a big group. You also learn new social skills. You don't have to pretend to be someone you aren't. You are with friends so you can be yourself. You don't have the pressure of keeping the conversation going. It also protects from tempting situations. If you haven't tried group dating, give it a chance. But remember, group dating does not isolate you from sexual pressures but it does lessen the risk.

Q. What do you do when you enjoy going out with a guy, but you feel that the relationship is getting too serious too fast?

A. The key is communication. Be honest with the guy and tell him how you feel. Assure him that you aren't rejecting him but let him know that you aren't as committed to the relationship as he is. Emphasize your desire to date as friends. If he can accept that, great. If not, tell him you may not be able to spend as much time with him in the future.

Q. What about going steady?

A. Going steady has its advantages. You no longer have to worry about getting a date. You find it easier to be yourself. You can develop closer friendships. You can learn to be more considerate.

But it also has its disadvantages. You can limit other friendships. You may tend to become possessive. You may tend to take each other for granted. Studies also show that going steady increases the chances of getting pregnant outside of marriage by 121 percent for whites and 91 percent for blacks (*The Journal of Marriage and Family*, Vol. 49, May 1987, p. 248).

It's not that going steady is wrong. It's just not always the wisest thing to do (adapted from *Dating: Picking (and Being) a Winner*, pp. 127–129).

Q. How do I break up with someone without hurting their feelings?

A. Breaking up is never easy, but it doesn't have to be a bloodbath. These suggestions will help you to handle it correctly.

Don't break up until you have settled down. If you are angry, wait until that feeling has subsided and you have confessed your anger to God and asked for His love.

Realize the potential hurt that breaking up can cause the other person. It can make him or her feel rejected or "not good enough," no matter how gentle you are. Think through how the other person may respond. Then do all you can to avoid adding to the pain. Also be sure to accept any responsibility that's yours for the relationship not working out (adapted from *Dating: Picking (and Being) a Winner*, pp. 138–142).

Q. My girlfriend just broke up with me. I feel like dying. What can I do?

A. Breaking up can bring confusion, loneliness, fear, depression and anger, just to name a few. Use the breaking-up experience to learn what you can do to become a better friend. Try to see their perspective of why they are breaking up. You may not agree with it but seek to understand it just the same. Thank them for the special times you've experienced. And assure them you do want to continue your friendship.

To help you during this rough time, try to change your focus by not talking or thinking much about your former sweetheart. Stay active and busy. You may want to avoid jumping quickly into another relationship. Allow your emotions time to get under control again.

Finally, remember that God is big enough to take care of all your dating concerns. Trust Him to bring you the man or woman of your dreams. If you wait on the best, God will always deliver.

6 Love

Q. *Is there such a thing as love at first sight?*

A. Love is not based on sight, looks or even romance. Real love is based upon commitment and a deep understanding of the other person. It is based on much more than just looks.

There is such a thing as *attraction* at first sight which can grow into real love. But *love,* a real, committed, true love cannot be determined at first sight.

Q. *I have such strong feelings for my boyfriend. Does that mean that I'm in love?*

A. Real love produces strong feelings. But strong feelings don't necessarily mean you are in love. Feelings come and go quickly, depending on what kind of mood you're in. To know if your love is real or not, avoid focusing on your feelings. Look instead at the depth of commitment you have for each other.

Q. *Isn't sex the ultimate expression of love?*

A. There are few things more beautiful than sex in the context of a loving marriage relationship. Sexual intercourse can be the most intimate expression of love. But sex as an expression of love is more the result of a committed marriage relationship than the cause of it. Sex was made for two people to enjoy and deepen their love in the protective bounds of marriage.

Q. *What's the difference between love and infatuation?*

A. Infatuation has been defined as "the emotional impulse of love, untested by time or circumstance." Since infatuation can lead to real love, sometimes it is difficult to see the difference. The characteristics in the chart on the next page show the differences between infatuation and real love.

Q. *What is real love?*

A. Have you ever noticed how often people use the word love to describe whether they like something or not? "I love to eat." "I love my new outfit." "I love the new girl in class even though I don't know her yet." "I love to do homework."

Trying to define real love can get pretty confusing. It helps to realize there are three different types of love.

The "If" kind of love says, "I love you if . . .

you do what I want you to do."
you treat me the way I think you should."
you meet all of my expectations."

"If" love is a conditional. It is committed to a person only as long as that person performs up to a certain standard. The moment that person's performance is unacceptable, "If" love is withdrawn.

"Because-of" love says, "I love you because . . .

you are great looking."
you treat me special."
you are the most popular person in school."

The Fairy Tale —Infatuation	The Real Thing —Love
Fall into it suddenly	Grows with time
Deepens little with time	Always deepening
Wants sex now	Willing to wait for sex
Up and down emotionally	Consistent
In love with love	In love with a person
Fickle	Faithful
Can't eat or sleep	Has proper perspective
Hostile break-up at the slightest irritations	Does not panic when problems arise
Emphasizes beauty	Emphasizes character
Gets	Gives
Based on my feelings	Based on other's needs
Self-centered	Self-controlled
Shows emotion	Shows devotion
Physical	Spiritual
Expects to find happiness	Expects to work at happiness
Asks "How am I doing?"	Asks "How are you doing?"
Focuses on the performance of the other person	Provides unconditional acceptance of the other person
May feel this way toward more than one person	Feels this way toward one and only one
Possessive	Allows the other person to relate to others
May be based on few contacts (only person you've dated)	Based on many contacts (dated many others)
Has an idealized image of the other person	Has a realistic view of the other person's strengths and weaknesses
Avoids problems	Works through problems

(Adapted from *Love: Making It Last*, pp. 18, 19.)

Now at first glance, nothing seems to be wrong with the "because-of" kind of love. Why wouldn't you like to go with a popular good-looking guy or gal who treated you special? The problem occurs when that person has an acne attack and his or her face breaks out into zit city, USA. Or there is an argument. Or they forget to call you. Or the biggie, some better looking, more popular and sweeter guy or gal comes along. If that happens, you can kiss "because-of" love bye-bye. It will be off chasing something or someone better.

"No-matter-what" kind of love, loves a person regardless of their looks, and loves them for who they are and who they are becoming. This kind of love is the real thing.

Q. *I'm dating a person who is frequently jealous of me. What can we do about it?*

A. Sometimes jealousy is intentionally provoked and the cause is obvious. Jealousy, however, can also occur in situations where there seems to be little basis for it. Where there is a frequent and strong manifestation of the emotion of jealousy, the real cause is usually the inadequacy and insecurity of the person with those feelings.

Some jealous people have excellent qualities— gentleness, sensitivity, graciousness, for example—and yet they are very insecure because of the problems from their background. If you yourself are secure and are willing to make a commitment to help such a person, through patience and open communication you can possibly help rebuild that person's sense of security and thereby reduce his or her jealousy.

Q. For several years I was involved in a serious relationship with a guy. Although the relationship is over, the pain is not. What can or should I do?

A. Feeling pain after a relationship has ended is normal and natural. It's good that you are able to admit your pain, but it's even more important to deal with it. Ending a serious relationship is much like losing a loved one through death. In most cases there is a similar period of grief and mourning in which tears may help your healing. But time will give you the distance to put your pain into perspective.

Try to avoid living in the past. Do not listen to "our song" or go to "our place." However, you need to realize that past emotions may continue for some time. You may still dream about your "ex." Don't let this confuse you. This does not prove that you're still in love, or that you'll never be able to love anyone else. It simply proves that you cared about the other person and that memories take time to fade and emotions take time to recover. It's important to avoid being overly critical of your "ex." Bitterness will only prolong your depression and encourage self-pity.

Q. I find myself very afraid of having any permanent relationship. I've been hurt too much in the past and I just can't seem to trust anyone else. Is there anything I can do?

A. Many persons of both sexes have been deeply hurt in past relationships to the extent that their capacity for trust has been seriously damaged. Since trust is such an essential part of a sound relationship, it's very important that you deal with your personal trust factor.

With God's help you can break your focus on the

past and its hurts. In time you can forgive others for not being perfect and for hurting you. As you forgive, emotional healing will come.

Q. I've experienced a lot of painful rejection. It's affecting my current relationship. Is it just me?

A. Many times a person seeking love and affection who finds only rejection may come to feel that he or she is unworthy or unacceptable as a person. The deeper these feelings grow, the more they focus on the past. Past experiences of frustration and disappointment can tend to make them feel insecure and fearful in every area of life, certain that the future holds only more hurt and pain. This, in turn, can erode self-esteem and hope.

Don't project your past experiences of rejection into the present. Dating or marital problems can develop when you think you've been rejected but you actually haven't been. You are reacting to past emotional experiences which have sensitized you in a way that makes you think you are again being rejected. It's important to be well enough in touch with your feelings so that you can be absolutely certain what causes these feelings of rejection. Being in touch with your feelings gives you a solid basis for determining whether you are actually experiencing rejection or simply replaying messages from the past.

Q. Does God have just one person picked out for me to marry, or does He have several possibilities for me to choose from?

A. This question has as many different answers as there are people you ask. Among the answers:

Things will just click.
You can't stand being apart.
You are compatible.
You will feel it deep in your heart.

It doesn't take a genius to decide which type of person you would enjoy spending the rest of your life with so, first, eliminate all noncontenders.

Then ask yourself the question: "Does God want me to marry *the* right person or *a* right person?" Some say God wants you to marry "the" right person, meaning He has one, and only one, person picked out for you to marry. Others feel that there are many people out there whom God would consider a suitable mate for you; therefore, God wants you to marry "a" right person.

To avoid the controversy and the confusion, consider this perspective: Of the rest, pick the best. Of all the contenders, pick the best one for you, then you have the best of both options. If God has only one picked out, you can be sure you got him or her. On the other hand, if there are several right ones out there, then you can be sure to get the best one possible (adapted from *Love: Making It Last,* pp. 123, 126).

Q. How can I know that I've found the right person to marry?

A. To know for certain if you've found the one for you, evaluate how long and how well you know each other. Real love is based on a thorough knowledge and understanding of the other person. If you find out in marriage your spouse is different from what he or she led you to believe, it's too late to back out. Anybody can pretend to be somebody that they aren't while dating. Once you're married, you can't pretend anymore. The real person comes out. Get to know that real person now. Make it a priority. Give it time.

Second, determine if the person loves you with "no matter what" love, (real love) and not just an "if" or "because of" kind of love. A great way to determine if you are loved this way is to read 1 Corinthians 13:4–8 and see if that's the way your prospective marriage partner loves you. To help you be objective, ask a friend if he agrees with your conclusions.

Finally, as with any major decision, take the necessary steps to discern if this is God's will for your life. The Bible will provide you with much needed guidance, but will not always give you a direct answer like, "Yes, it is God's will for you to marry Fred Ferd." One of the best places to get specific direction is from your parents.

Most parents love their children and want to see them happy, both now and in the future. They have the advantage of experience and can give you valuable insights in making the right choice.

One final thought, keep in mind that you should be more concerned with *being* the right person than *finding* the right person. Major on becoming the kind of person who would make a great husband or wife.

Q. Is there anything wrong with an interracial marriage?

A. The question of interracial marriage is both complex and sensitive. From a biblical and moral point of view, there is no reason you shouldn't marry someone of another race or ethnic background—provided he or she is also a believer.

However, here are some issues you need to consider. All research to date has shown that the greater the cultural differences, the less chance there is for proper marital adjustment. Background, social status, and family customs are all important factors to take into consideration.

Interracial marriages can create problems for children. They may feel rejected and excluded by other children as they grow up.

Certainly the above barriers can be overcome. Any successful marriage requires a great deal of commitment, effort and maturity. An interracial marriage may require a greater degree of effort and maturity. This is why many marriage experts feel that while Scripture is clear that interracial marriages are fine and acceptable, it may be difficult in your culture. You should seek wise counsel before making the final decision. Weigh your parents' feelings and counsel carefully. Their insights can help you more objectively balance your own feelings.

Q. Should couples who are planning to be married confess to each other any and all previous sexual experiences?

A. Openness and transparency should characterize your relationship in all matters including your past. However, you should use wisdom and discretion in sharing past sexual experiences. Avoid going into unnecessary detail.

You may want to say something like this. "There was

a point in my life when I had problems but God has rebuilt moral purity into my life and I have not compromised since.

"I want you to know that I love you and assure you of my faithfulness in the future."

If your prospective marriage partner cannot accept your past, now is the time to find out. It is to be hoped that Romans 15:7 will characterize his or her attitude. "Wherefore, accept one another, just as Christ also accepted us to the glory of God."

Don't be surprised if your prospective mate asks you to go get tested to determine if you have an STD (sexually transmitted disease). Because of the rampage of AIDS (Acquired Immune Deficiency Syndrome) people are concerned that they may marry someone who is infected but shows no signs.

Q. My parents are reluctant to give their blessing for us to get married. They say we have too many problems to work out. Wouldn't it be easier to solve them once we got married?

A. *No way!* Listen carefully to your mom and dad. They definitely know what they are talking about.

One of the best things about getting married is you no longer have to tell each other good-bye and go home. One of the hardest things about marriage is adjusting to the differences each one brings to the relationship. The vast majority of young couples have an extremely difficult time getting along with each other during that first year of marriage. And that includes those couples who didn't have any problems initially.

Unfortunately, you probably can't imagine how

much more difficult the adjustment period becomes if you bring existing problems from the past into the marriage. The tendency is to think your love or feelings can work through it all. Possibly so, but the chances are very slim.

When you get married you want every chance possible that it will succeed. You want to stay married once you get married. To maximize those chances, work out your problems ahead of time.

Q. *How can I know if my love is mature enough to make a relationship last?*

A. Following are ten things characteristic of mature love. Check them out and measure your own love.

A. Mature love is total-person oriented.
B. Mature love is spelled G-I-V-E.
C. Mature love shows respect.
D. Mature love has no conditions.
E. Mature love experiences joy in being together.
F. Mature love is realistic.
G. Mature love has a protective attitude.
H. Mature love takes responsibility.
I. Mature love is demonstrated in commitment.
J. Mature love never stops growing.

Determining the level of your "love maturity" isn't always easy. When trying to decide whether your love is mature enough to marry someone, remember these key factors:

Don't ignore your feelings of doubt.

Don't be pressured because you fear you won't find someone as nice as this person.

Can you really enjoy this person apart from the physical?

Not being able to have a mature love for one person doesn't mean you can't find a mature love for another person.

Q.   I have been dating this girl for some time, and I think that she is the "right one" for me. However, she doesn't agree. I would really like to marry her. What can I do?

A.   Successful and satisfying dating relationships are certainly not easy for anyone to achieve. The problem you are experiencing is called "uneven commitment." You have a relationship in which one party is much more serious and interested than the other. Several basic causes exist for this kind of a situation. For example, a person may enter a relationship simply because it's convenient. For some, a dating relationship can be a means of dealing with loneliness. For others it can be a ticket to dinners and entertainment. Now that does not necessarily mean that the other party is being "used." It depends on one's expectations. Did you expect more than a casual relationship? Were those expectations realistic?

You may feel that the other person really loves you, when in reality the actions and attitudes of the other person do not show that. Real love has a sense of mutuality and oneness. A couple with the "real thing" sees themselves as a unit. Each feels fully wanted, accepted, and secure. This kind of a relationship is not one-sided or uneven.

So what can you do about it? Simply this: be very cautious in a one-sided or uneven relationship. If you feel strongly about the relationship, then have a heart-to-heart talk with the other person and bring the situation out into the open. If you do not receive a positive response in words or attitude, then it is likely that the relationship does not have the elements to make it lasting and meaningful.

Q. My boyfriend and I believe we are to get married and we already have our parents' permission. How long should our engagement be?

A. Different couples have different needs, but two guidelines will help you pick the best length.

The engagement should last long enough to prepare. Two big events need preparation, the wedding ceremony and life together after the ceremony. Planning the wedding ceremony usually takes three to six months, depending on the size of the ceremony. The premarital counseling should last about three months if you don't have difficult problems to work through.

Q. We recently got engaged. What do we do during this time?

A. Engagement is an in-between time. You are no longer dating, but you aren't married yet either. During your engagement, think through the ingredients involved in a successful marriage. Talk, study and decide how your marriage will handle conflict, finances, praying together, communication, in-laws, children, the dividing up of responsibilities, etc. By doing so your adjustment period will be much easier.

7 Sex

Q. Is sex dirty?

A. Sex is definitely not dirty. When God created the world, He looked at it and declared that everything was good. That included sex! God created sex as a good and enjoyable aspect of our lives.

God isn't down on sex. After all, He made it. God designed the gift of sex to be enjoyed within marriage. Hebrews 13:4 says, "Marriage should be honored by all, and the marriage bed kept pure, for God will judge the adulterer and all the sexually immoral."

There's nothing more beautiful than sex between two people committed to one another in marriage. To see the healthy view of the Bible on sex, read Proverbs 5:18–19.

Q. Why is the Bible against sex?

A. Of all those in church, 80 to 90 percent, young and old, think the Bible has a negative view of sex.

The Bible is not against sex. There's not a single verse in the Bible that calls sex sin. There's not one verse in the Bible against sex or that says sex is wrong or dirty.

Now, don't misunderstand, there are many passages in the Bible that speak against the misuse of sex, of sexual expression outside of the loving commitment of marriage. It is not sex but rather the misuse of sex that the Bible calls fornication, adultery, etc.

Q. Does the Bible teach that pre-marital sex is wrong?

A. Two specific passages speak about the sin of fornication, which means voluntary sex between an unmarried person and someone of the opposite sex.

In 1 Corinthians 7:2, the apostle Paul writes that one reason for marriage (certainly not the only reason) is to avoid fornication. "To avoid fornication let every man have his own wife, and let every woman have her own husband."

Paul gives the same basic advice in 1 Thessalonians 4:3-5, "For this is the will of God, even your sanctification, that you abstain from immorality (fornication); that each one of you know how to take a wife for himself in holiness and honor, not in the passion of lust like heathen who do not know God."

In each passage, Paul warns unmarried people about the temptation toward immorality (fornication). He advocates marriage as an antidote to a single life of premarital sexual relations.

Q. But what about living together? Isn't that really almost the same thing as being married?

A. Living together is not at all the same as marriage. The quality and degree of the marriage commitment is much different than a commitment just to live together. Not only are the marriage vows made officially and publicly, but they are made "for better or for worse, in sickness and in health, as long as you both shall live."

You've probably heard that living together can help two people find out whether they are compatible for marriage. They reason that by testing the relationship beforehand, failure and divorce can be avoided. However, there are so many couples who thought themselves compatible while living together, but once married discovered something had happened to their compatibility. In fact, recent research shows that live-together couples are more likely to separate and divorce than those who wait until marriage to set up a joint household (*The Boston Globe*, "Study Finds No Marriage Insurance in Cohabitation," Irene Sego, 7/3/89).

Q. Why do we have such strong sexual feelings if premarital sex is wrong?

A.   God has placed inside every person a strong desire for sex. He wants you to have it. Which may make you wonder why He made your desires so powerful if you can't enjoy them right now. Is God playing a cosmic joke on you?

Not at all. Be thankful you have that strong desire. You also need to realize that because people today mature physically during their early teens and often don't marry until their early to late twenties, there are years and years of struggle to keep your desires under control.

It hasn't always been that way. Until the last 100 years or so, people generally married within a year or two after they reached physical maturity. Today, you have a tough course to run. Our sex-saturated society doesn't help much either.

But remember, God has given you all the power you need to keep your sexual desires under control. Following His advice in 2 Timothy 2:22 will help: "Flee the evil desires of youth, and pursue righteousness, faith, love and peace, along with those who call on the Lord out of a pure heart."

Q. *Is homosexuality an acceptable alternative lifestyle?*

A. A growing number of people are accepting homosexuality as a normal form of sexual expression. The Bible does speak to this subject. Check out Leviticus 18:22, Romans 1:26–32, and 1 Corinthians 6:9–11.

We believe that God intended love and marriage to be between a man and a woman. While some men and women may be attracted to the same sex, we don't believe any sexual involvement between them is biblically acceptable.

Q. *Can I have premarital sex and still be a Christian?*

A. We'll turn the question back to you. Have you slipped just once, or is having sex a continuing pattern in your life?

It's always possible for a Christian to sin, but you need to seriously examine your life if you are sinning habitually. First John 2:4 says, "The one who says, 'I have come to know Him; and does not keep His commandments, is a liar, and the truth is not in him.'"

Q. *How far is too far?*

A. Have you ever wondered how far sexually it was OK to go? If so, you're not the first guy or girl to ask the question, "How far is too far?"

Most kids are looking for someone with "authority" to step up and draw a hard and fast line and say, "OK, everything up to here is fine. But if you go past this point, as a Christian, you are out of God's will." It sounds nice and simple, but it doesn't work that way.

Actually, how far is too far is not the best question to

ask. There are better questions to ask like: "What caring actions can I use to show my true feelings to my date? What actions express how much I care about my date at this point in our relationship?" These are a lot different than wondering how far you can go to satisfy your physical desires. It's not so much "How far is too far?" but "What is honest, righteous and best for where we are right now?" The Bible is clear about drawing a line when it says, ". . . that no man transgress and defraud his brother . . ." (1 Thess. 4:6).

To work this out in real life, let's consider several things.

First, get in touch with the reasons why you do things. It usually starts so slowly that you don't realize it's happening, but when either one begins to raise their own physical desires above what is right and spiritually healthy for the other person, they've crossed an important "line."

Second, apply the basic biblical commandment to "love one another" to the situation. We're not talking sex here. We're talking the 1 Corinthians, Chapter 13, verses four through seven kind of love which unselfishly seeks out God's very best for another. That person you're dating is more than a friend, lover, or whatever else—they are a child of God, special and precious in His sight. Not treating them as such crosses that line as well. To see if you're acting in a loving way, replace the word love each time it's used in 1 Corinthians 13:4–7 with your name. (i.e., Steve is kind. Steve is patient.)

Third, recognize that the reason physical affection between a guy and girl is so exciting is because God made it to be that way. And it is progressive in nature—one stage always naturally leads to the next. God placed the expression of sexual affection in the loving context of a husband and wife's relationship in marriage. Read carefully Proverbs 5:17–21.

Recently, I (Josh) helped a high school girl figure out a chart on this progression. It was a project for her sex education class. I think that you'll find the diagram we made up interesting and helpful. Here it is:

The Road to Sexual Arousal and Intercourse

Abstinence

Necking

Holding hands
Hugging
Casual kissing (peck kissing)

—— The Line ——

Prolonged kissing

Light Petting	French kissing (including last stages of necking—ears, neck) Breasts covered Breasts bared

Heavy Petting	Genitals covered Genitals bared Oral sex Genital to genital

Intercourse

Now note that we've drawn a line labeled "The Line." You wanted an honest answer to "How far is too far?" Well, for whatever our personal opinion is worth, here it is. We don't believe couples in a dating relationship, whatever their age, can progress much beyond this point without asking for trouble. If you and your date are honestly committed to saving sex for marriage, you need to realize that past this line you begin to arouse in each other desires that cannot be righteously fulfilled outside of marriage. That gets us back to convictions again.

Setting your standards and "drawing your lines" will enable you to stand up in a situation requiring serious resisting. They will keep you from making a mistake you may later regret.

Q. Is it okay to kiss each other?

A. It depends on what you mean by kissing. There are two main kinds of kisses. First, you have the overseas type, you know the kind, where the water flies all over the place. This kind, commonly called French kissing, differs greatly from the ordinary American kiss—the kind of kiss you might give your sister when you are in a good mood.

If you read the Bible much, you know that God isn't against kissing. All through the New Testament He encourages you to greet one another with a holy kiss (Rom. 16:16; 1 Cor. 16:20; 2 Cor. 13:12; 1 Thess. 5:26; 1 Peter 5:14). So if you really want to be Scriptural in your dating, when you greet each other at the door, kiss. When you let her in the car and you go around the other side to get in, you are greeting her again! So kiss again. You take her to the McRestaurant, sit her at the

McTable, go get your McBurgers from the McCounter, bring them back to your McDate, you are greeting her again! So give her a McKiss.

God isn't down on kissing. But He wants your kisses to be holy. So the question is, "What does a French kiss do to your body?" Be honest. If you say, "Nothing," then you haven't yet reached puberty.

Q. Is pornography wrong?

A. You're hanging around the locker room and you see a rapid gathering of guys and a lot of laughs. You walk over, and they tell you to take a look at this. Then they jam a 12 × 12 full-color photo of a naked woman in your face.

What happens, guys? Your body goes berserk!

Many students, guys and girls, are into pornography, whether it's the sexy picture hanging on the wall or the magazines stacked under the mattress (not a very good hiding place). In fact, in one survey 99 percent of the young men and 91 percent of the young women had read or looked at pornographic magazines.

Pornography treats men and women as sex objects. It cheapens sex. Even more, it can get a hold on your mind and dominate your thoughts, so you are drawn to pornography any time you become lonely or sexually stimulated.

Q. What about masturbation? Is it wrong, or is it a gift from God?

A. The basic problem with masturbation is what you do with your mind. You may begin with lustful thought. You may be looking at some kind of suggestive or pornographic material. Or, you may even fantasize yourself with a guy or gal you wish to go out with. The point is, if you have lustful thoughts during masturbation, it is wrong.

The solution is to bring your thought life under the control of the Holy Spirit, realizing that your mind is your most important sex organ. In Romans 12:2, Paul tells us, "Do not be conformed to this world, but be transformed by the renewing of your mind." As a Christian you should be in a continuing process renewing your mind. As you renew your mind, with the help of the Holy Spirit, you will experience more and more victory over sexual temptation and lust. Another potential problem is that you program yourself for immediate sexual gratification and that could eventually cause difficulty in your marriage.

Q. Are lustful thoughts wrong, or just when they become actions?

A. In Matthew 5:27, 28 Jesus explained lust clearly: "You have heard that it was said, 'Do not commit adultery.' But I tell you that anyone who looks at a woman lustfully has already committed adultery with her in his heart."

That is a strong statement. Obviously Jesus didn't take lust lightly. The word He uses in the Greek is *epithumia*. *Epi* means "over" and *thumos* means "passion." Lust means overpassion. (Now you can say you know a foreign language.) Lust is a burning desire for the opposite sex beyond the boundaries God set for the sexual relationship.

God has blessed you with your sexual desires. He has special plans for you to use those desires within marriage. That is normal. So when you look at a person and say, "Now there's an attractive person," that's okay.

But sexual desires that come from lust are not healthy. If you think, I wonder what he (or she) looks like undressed, you're headed toward lust. From there your thoughts can run out of control until you imagine anything from messing around to having sexual intercourse with a person, and those thoughts are wrong (adapted from *Sex: Desiring the Best*, St. Clair/Jones, HLP).

Q. If lust is only in your mind, can it really hurt you?

A. Proverbs 6:25, 27 compares lust to a fire: "Do not lust in your heart after her beauty or let her captivate you with her eyes. Can a man scoop fire into his lap without his clothes being burned?" Picture your eyes catching on fire, then the fire spreading to your mind, then consuming your body. Fire begins with your eyes.

Your eyes are bombarded with lust-producing material all the time. One youth leader said, "We live in a sex-saturated society that constantly bombards all of us with erotic stimuli. Suggestive poses and near-nude bodies are just a glance away. 'Come on' eyes peer at us from colorful, provocative ads on television, in magazines, and on billboards."

If lust catches fire in your eyes, then it can spread to your mind, and your mind is your most important sex organ. If the fire of lust smolders there, you are in trouble. It's only a matter of time until the fire explodes into your body. Your body then blazes with lust, not because of what you have done, but because of what you have seen and what you have thought about it.

Stop the fire from ever catching hold in your mind by protecting your eyes. Thousands of years before Jesus, Job said, "I have made a covenant with my eyes not to look lustfully at a girl." We can't offer any better advice (adapted from *Sex: Desiring the Best*, St. Clair/ Jones, HLP).

Q. *Does the way girls dress affect guys?*

A. We've asked guys why they thought girls dressed the way they do. Their answer: 1) to be in fashion; 2) to get attention; 3) to obtain acceptance; and 4) to be considered attractive or sexy.

Generally, when a guy sees a girl dressed in a way that accentuates her body, especially the legs, hips, and breasts, his hormones start hopping. So how a girl dresses does affect guys.

That's why the Bible says whether you're a guy or girl, dress modestly. It doesn't mean you can't dress in fashion, but you need to do it in modesty.

Here are some questions to ask. Do you dress to draw someone's attention to you as a person, or to your body? Do you dress to cause sensual awareness of you? Do you dress so a guy or girl thinks you would be a good mate or a good one-time date? Only you can answer these questions.

One way to help, is for the guys and girls from your church youth group to hold each other accountable for their dress. Guys should ask girls, "Is this too much, too little, or just right?" Girls should do the same. When you do, you will get honest answers, but not always the answers you want to hear. As you do this, you will learn what clothes draw attention to your face and which ones draw attention to your figure.

Q. *How can I get lustful thoughts under control?*

A. Ephesians 4:22–23 tells us, "You were taught, with regard to your former way of life, to put off your old self, which is being corrupted by its deceitful desires; to be made new in the attitude of your minds."

You can renew your mind by replacing lustful thoughts with pure thoughts. From your chemistry class you know that a liquid forces gas out of a test tube. In the same way, pure thoughts can force lustful thoughts out of your mind. When your mind begins to wander, immediately replace your lustful thoughts with pure thoughts.

You can do that in many ways—Christian music and magazines, books, good conversations. The most significant way is through Scripture memory.

To memorize Scripture:

Decide to memorize at least one verse per week. Start with these: Romans 12:1, 2; Psalm 51:10; Colossians 3:1–3; Psalm 119:9, 11; 1 Corinthians 10:13; Philippians 4:8.

Memorize word for word. Don't make up your own translation.

Think about the verse. This is called meditation. Ask what this verse means and what God is saying to you through this verse.

Apply the verse to your life. "As a result of this verse, I will. . . ."

Review. Go over the new verse every day for two months. Then once a week after that.

Q. *It doesn't make sense to wait until marriage to have sex; what difference does it make?*

A. Any time God warns you not to do something, He's trying to take care of you.

He wants to protect you from a variety of negative consequences. He also wants to make sure you can enjoy the tremendous benefits that come from obedience.

Physically, He wants to protect you from the damage that the fifty different kinds of sexually transmitted diseases can cause you. More than one million teenage girls get pregnant every year. He doesn't want you to be one of them and live with the heartache and problems that pregnancy creates.

Emotionally, He wants to guard you from the negative emotions that plague a person involved in sex before marriage. Fears like "What if my parents find out?" "What if we break up?" "What if we get caught?" Guilt that comes the morning after. Shame from being known as "easy" or "cheap." Doubt about your self-image, your relationship with God, and whether you're being loved for yourself or used for your body.

Relationally, God wants to protect you from breakdowns in communication. Often, your relationship can concentrate on sex, rather than on each other. While you used to talk, now you just make out. Although most people don't realize it, you carry all your past experiences and relationships into your future marriage, which can create problems. Your spouse may feel super-insecure, always wondering if you're comparing him or her to your past partners.

Spiritually, not only can you blow your testimony on campus—because people might find out—but also you'll feel like God is a million miles away. You've damaged your fellowship with Him, and with other committed Christians, because you'll feel like a hypocrite.

God wants to make sure you get the best, so He warns you to wait. By waiting, you'll guarantee your physical health, emotional maturity, relational happiness, and spiritual growth. You can't win by jumping the starting gun for sex. And you can't lose when you follow God's ways (adapted from *Why Wait?*, McDowell/Day, HLP).

Q.   I recently found out I'm pregnant. What do I do?

A. Pregnancy happens to hundreds of thousands of teenagers every year. Chances are great that one of your friends is in that situation right now. If you are pregnant you have some major decisions to make. You need to look at all your options, and make some tough choices.

The first thing to do is to seek help. You don't need to go through this alone. Find someone you can trust. Go to your parents if you can. With good Christ-centered counseling your options will become clear. While you will have some very hard choices to make, let us assure you there is a life after an unplanned pregnancy.

Q.   Has the emphasis on safe sex put a stop to sexually transmitted diseases?

A. What is happening is startling. Even with all the emphasis on safe sex, syphillis has exploded: a 30 percent increase in 9 months. This doesn't even take into account herpes, AIDS, gonorrhea, and the 50 other sexually transmitted diseases (STD's).

One of the worst epidemics in the history of the U.S. was the polio epidemic of the 1950s. But in the last twelve months, one year, more little babies have been born with a birth defect because of an STD than all the children combined affected by polio during the entire ten-year epidemic of the 1950s. It's the babies now who are paying the price for "free love."

One out of every four sexually active women in universities now has chalmydia trachomatous, the number one STD. Four million will get it this year. Of the primary strain 25 percent of the women become sterile, 33 percent of babies will be born with it, and, of the major strain, 13 out of every 100 babies born will be born with a major birth defect, mainly blindness, because of CT.

Don't be fooled into thinking there's such a thing as "safe sex" outside of a faithful marriage relationship. There isn't.

Q. How can I warn my friends about all these dangers?

A. One of your friends comes up to you and says this weekend could be the big one. Your friend thinks she might have sex with her boyfriend and asks your advice and support.

We hope we've given you enough relevant information and ideas to help you discuss with your friend the positive points of waiting. Don't try to convince your friend with the negatives. Instead, point out the advantages of waiting. Think about asking your friend to write down five advantages and five disadvantages of having sex before going ahead with it.

If this doesn't affect your friend, loan this book to your friend and point out the pages and questions that have helped you.

Q. How do I say no to sexual pressure?

A. *Set standards beforehand.* Determine your standards, Then make sure your friends know about them before the date.

Be accountable. This means you have another person

whom you keep informed about how pure you are staying in your own actions, thoughts, and attitudes. This person usually is someone more mature spiritually, someone you respect. If you start to slide, he or she loves you enough to help you get back on track.

Let your lifestyle show. By your conversations, your body language, and your actions, you can say no to sexual permissiveness.

Keep your mind pure. What you feed your mind determines what you think about, so it is important to be careful with what you let your eyes see.

Avoid sexually oriented media. Media includes movies, television, magazines.

Dress to reflect your convictions. Modesty in your dress is important for girls and guys. Wear clothes that look good, but that aren't designed to turn on your date.

Choose your companions carefully. Hang around with people who have the same values and convictions that you have. Get involved in groups that support you in your values.

Seek the wisdom of others. Choose good role models. Scripture teaches that "there is much wisdom in much counsel or advice." Confusing emotions can get sorted out as you talk with older, more mature people.

Ask God to help. None of these other strategies will work unless you realize that you really do need help. God doesn't want you to be a lone ranger. Use prayer as your first step and all along the way.

Break off the relationship. If you're getting pressured or giving in to pressure, you can relieve the pressure right away by breaking off the dating relationship.

Look for the way of escape. God promises that He will show you the way out of temptation.

Make a fast, strategic exit. Be honest about your weakness. If you think you can't handle it or you've given in to this situation before, head for the door (adapted from *Why Wait?*, McDowell/Day, HLP).

Q. What does God think of you after you've lost your virginity?

A. So great is God's love that He can give you a gift that no amount of money can buy—spiritually restored virginity.

Picture God looking out of heaven through a microscope at you—your life is on a biology slide under the microscope. He sees all the bad things you have ever done, including when you lost your virginity. Then you invited Jesus into your life and turned from your sin. Now all God sees is Jesus Christ in you, and Jesus is perfect. Because Jesus lives in you, God sees you just as He does His Son: perfect.

The apostle Paul explains how God restores your virginity spiritually: "He [God] chose us in Him [Christ], before the foundation of the world, that we should be holy and blameless before Him" (Eph. 1:4). Wow! When God looks at you, all He sees is that you are "holy and blameless"—in the right relationship with God.

Perhaps you're thinking, "What about *my* sin?" Ephesians 1:7–8 says, "So overflowing is his kindness towards us that he took away all our sins through the blood of his Son, by whom we are saved; and he showered down upon us the richness of his grace—for how well he understands us and knows what is best for us at all time."

Wow! No matter how badly you sinned or how many

times, Christ offers you the gift of total forgiveness and total healing—spiritually restored virginity.

There is only one way to have the gift. Receive it. First John 1:9 tells how, "If we confess our sins, he is faithful and just and will forgive us our sins and purify us from all unrighteousness."

If you are not sure you have accepted God's forgiveness for any sexual sin, this prayer may help: "Lord Jesus, I have messed up my sex life. I admit that I sinned against You. I turn away from my sin. Right now I receive Your love and forgiveness. I am no longer dirty, sinful or guilty. I am clean, holy, and blameless because of Jesus Christ. Thank You for the precious gift of spiritually restored virginity. In Jesus' name, Amen" (adapted from *Sex: Desiring the Best*, St. Clair/Jones, HLP).

Q. I love my girlfriend and know she is the one for me, but she just told me she isn't a virgin. What should I do?

A. If I had the opportunity to get married and had to choose between two women—both believers, one a physical virgin but not really sensitive to God, the other not a physical virgin but one who has confessed and repented of her sin and is sensitive to God—I wouldn't even have to think about it. I would marry the lady who's not a virgin but is sensitive to God. You don't love a person for her past, you love someone for who she is right now.

Q. I've blown it sexually. Can God ever use me again?

A. Have you ever tried to convince someone that something really happened? That can be frustrating, especially if they were there when it happened but just can't remember. That's the way it is trying to talk with God about your sin once He has forgiven you.

Any time you sin, Satan wants you to feel worthless and unworthy of God's love and forgiveness. If he can keep you feeling vaguely guilty and condemned, he can keep you from loving God and helping others.

God, on the other hand, takes your sin, puts it on Jesus Christ, and completely forgets it. If you bring it up in conversation, He won't even know what you're talking about. It's not on the records.

What you need to concentrate on now is letting God build purity in your life as you obey Him in every area of your life.

Paul has the best advice, "Brothers, I do not consider myself yet to have taken hold of it. But one thing I do: Forgetting what is behind and straining toward what is ahead, I press on toward the goal to win the prize for which God has called me heavenward in Christ Jesus" (Phil. 3:13, 14).

8   *Abuse*

Q. How common is sexual abuse?

A. One out of every three girls and one in seven guys will be sexually assaulted before they reach the age of eighteen! But more than half of the victims will not tell anyone within a year of the assault. Most of them feel guilty and cover up the sexual abuse.

Perhaps even more alarming is the attitudes many guys have about sexual abuse and assault. A national study of 1,700 sixth to ninth grade students revealed that:

- 65 percent of today's students say it is acceptable for a man to rape a girl (force her to have sex) if they've been dating for more than six months.
- 25 percent said it was acceptable to rape a girl if a guy spends money on her.
- 87 percent said it was acceptable for a husband to rape his wife.

Over a three-year period, 6,100 undergraduates were surveyed on 32 college campuses with these results:

- 1 in 4 women surveyed were victims of rape or attempted rape.
- 84 percent of those raped knew their attackers.
- 57 percent of the rapes happened on dates.

- 75 percent of the men and 55 percent of the women involved in date rapes had been drinking or taking drugs before the attack.
- 42 percent of the rape victims told no one about the attack.
- Only 5 percent reported their rapes to the police or sought help at a rape crisis center.
- 42 percent of the women who had been raped and 55 percent of the men who committed a rape said they had sex again with their victims.
- 84 percent of the men who committed rape said that what they did was definitely not rape.

And finally, a survey among 247 females at a Christian liberal arts college found that at least 19 percent of all the females on campus had been abused before the age of eighteen.

The chances are great that there are, even in your church youth group, other kids who have been sexually abused. Some may be in the midst of continuing abuse. Or you may be a victim.

Q. What does it mean to be sexually abused?

A. Sexual abuse can happen in many different ways. Someone could indecently expose themselves to you; you could receive an obscene phone call; you could be aware that you have been seen by a peeping tom; or if you are under age eighteen, an adult could fondle you sexually or force you to have sex. A violent form of sexual abuse is rape. Another form of abuse is incest, sexual relations of any kind with a family member to whom you're not married.

About 41 percent of the abusers in the United States

are friends or acquaintances, 27 percent are strangers, and 23 percent are relatives (incest). In fact, nearly 75 percent of all rape and sexual assaults are committed by people known to the victims (*Youthworker Journal*, Winter 1985).

Q. What is incest?

A. Incest is intimate sexual contact between a child under the age of eighteen and a relative such as an uncle, aunt, brother, sister, stepbrother, stepsister, mother, father, stepmother, stepfather, or grandparent. In other words, someone you are not legally allowed to marry. About 23 percent of all sexual abuse is incest.

Father-daughter incest is the most commonly reported and legally prosecuted form. In about one quarter of the reported cases, sexual contact is a one-time occurrence, but more typically it continues over a period of years, having an average time span of three and a half years.

When the daughter is young, between five and twelve, the relationship very rarely includes actual intercourse. Once the daughter is past twelve, intercourse is likely to be part of the sexual contact. Alcohol is a significant factor. (Between 20 and 50 percent of the fathers are alcoholics. Even when the man is not an alcoholic, the first experience may take place when he has been drinking.)

A number of studies have concluded that brother-sister incest is the most common form of incest. Research does not support the view that brother-sister incest is "normal." It usually occurs in families where serious problems exist.

Healthy families exhibit a lot of holding and affection. However, affection is different from deliberate erotic stimulation (*Redbook*, 11/80, pp. 83–86).

Q. What is rape or date rape?

A. Rape occurs when sexual intercourse or oral sex is forced on you against your will. This could be by someone you know or by a complete stranger. Nearly 75 percent of all rape and sexual assault is done by a person known to the victim.

Date rape occurs when intercourse or oral sex is forced on you by the person you are dating. The force does not have to involve a weapon or even the threat of physical harm. It can be trying to overpower a victim physically. It can also involve intimidating threats like, "Hey, if you don't want to put out, you can get out of the car right now and walk home."

Rape or date rape is a violent crime and it's against the law. Yet you've probably heard some people say, "They brought it on themselves by the way they acted or dressed." That's wrong! No one has the right to rape another person, no matter what she's done! If someone forces sex on you, you're the victim and he's the law-breaker. Remember, forced sex is not love; it's a crime!

Q. Should I tell someone if I'm being abused?

A. Because sexually abusing someone is against the law, speak up! Decide to tell someone the truth about what happened—a trusted friend, your pastor, a counselor, a doctor. In most states the person you tell is required to tell the local authorities. That's because all of us want sexual abuse to stop. And what about you—the victim? You need to be protected so it won't happen again.

And think of this: telling the truth may help stop the person from abusing you again or someone else. Telling can also be a help to you. One abuse victim said, "It is such a relief to know I don't have to hide any part of my life and to know that people accept me for what I am."

But telling isn't easy either. What if some people won't believe you? If the abuser is someone you care about, it can be confusing. You could be feeling anger and resentment toward the person and yet have some good memories and even love for them. It takes a lot of courage to speak out. Remember, the first step toward solving the deep problems of the abuser is for him (or her) to be forced to confront the problems. Your testimony can help start the healing process for the abuser.

Keeping your feelings inside may only make matters worse. If you don't get out and deal with it, the effects of abuse could go on for many years. Family relationships could become strained and painful. You could become afraid of getting close with someone else. Some people act out their confusion in various ways such as drinking, using drugs, or abusing food.

Some churches and communities have specialists in the area of helping the victims of sexual abuse and rape. Ask your school counselor, doctor, teacher, pastor, one of your parents' friends, or one of your own parents to help you locate help in the community.

Q. What can I do to avoid being date raped or sexually abused?

A. If you are in a situation where you have been sexually abused or fear that you may be, there are a number of practical steps you can take to better secure your safety. And that should be your first goal.

Try to avoid being alone with the abuser or anyone who wants to touch you in a sexual way. If you are uncomfortable around someone—maybe you feel fear about something and you don't even know why—trust your instincts. Avoid being alone with that person.

Don't deny that the abuse hurts you and you are angry about it. Talk to a trusted friend about the way you are feeling. Your feelings are not abnormal or weird; they are very normal.

Sexual pressure of any kind is wrong. You never owe sex to anyone no matter what the other person has done for you.

Set an example of how to treat guys and girls by mutually respecting each other.

Date only people you know. Blind dates are always risky, simply because you don't know the other person. Become friends before you go out alone on a date with someone. Not only will you get to know something about the person's character, but your date will come to know you more as a person and not just a sex object.

Group dates with more than one couple could be helpful. An abuser or rapist usually needs to isolate his victim.

Don't go "parking." Avoid isolated situations or places.

Don't go into each other's home alone.

Respect others. Talking about or looking at another person in a way that makes her uncomfortable is not cool—it violates a person's dignity. Don't join in with friends who violate—verbally or physically—another person.

Believe that when someone says no to sex, he or she means no! Honor another person's words.

Q. I've been sexually abused in the past. How can I deal with all the feelings I'm having?

A. The emotional effects of sexual abuse can be very long lasting. Sometimes they are disguised in other symptoms. If you were abused in your past, you might ask yourself the following questions:

Do I often feel hopeless, alone, and believe I am a burden to others?

Do I find myself withdrawing from family and friends?

Have I been having trouble concentrating lately?

Am I having trouble handling my work or school assignments?

Do I feel I have to keep "the secret"?

If you have been abused or raped and you answered yes to any of these questions, you are having a normal reaction. People who have experienced sexual abuse often have these feelings.

One abused person said, "I live in a dark, dark cavern of fear and isolation and guilt." You may feel very confused or fear that you won't be believed if you tell someone. If the abuser is someone you care about, you are probably having mixed and confusing feelings of anger, hate, resentment, as well as more positive feelings such as love, good memories, and hopeful promises.

These feelings need to be acknowledged, talked through, and resolved.

Keeping these feelings bottled up inside may only make the problem worse. Anger is a normal reaction to a loss—whether it's a physical loss or an emotional loss. All sexual abuse victims feel anger and need to express it in healthy ways. You don't have to be angry all the time. You can begin to take charge of your life. You can learn to trust your own judgment and get close to others and yet remain in control. This process may take years, but there is definite hope for you. Pastors, counselors, your doctor, a support group, or trusted friends can provide you much help as you struggle to get free from your past experiences.

Q. What do I do if I have been sexually abused?

A. You must realize that it was not your fault. It was a criminal act against you. God does not condemn you. You are not "spoiled" or "dirty" in any way.

The effects of abuse may influence your relationships over a long period of time. But you can recognize when this is happening and learn what you can do about it. You can recover. There is healing for you.

Reach out to trusted friends. Call them on the phone and tell them you need to talk, or go see them.

Reach out to God. Talk to Him as you would your best friend. He is always there to listen and care. The Bible says, "Pour out your hearts to Him, for God is our refuge" (Ps. 62:8) and "Cast all your anxiety on Him because He cares for you" (1 Peter 5:7).

If the feelings get too tough to handle, start a journal by writing out how you feel at that moment. If you're afraid someone will read your notes, tear them up after you're finished or put them in a safe place.

There is hope—for you and for the abuser. It is never too late to ask for help. God promises to heal wounds. One special promise can be found in 1 Peter 5:10, "The God of all grace, who called you to His eternal glory in Christ, after you have suffered a little while, will Himself restore you and make you strong, firm, and steadfast."

Here are some other promises from God that you can claim.

God can heal your hurts. "He heals the broken-hearted. He bandages their wounds" (Ps. 147:3).

You are a delight to God. "Because He delights in me, He saved me" (Ps. 18:19).

God is your protector. "God is our protection and our strength. He always helps in times of trouble" (Ps. 46:1).

God chose you to be His child. ". . . He chose us before the world was made. In His love He chose us . . ." (Eph. 1:4).

God loves you and has a wonderful plan for your life. "I know what I have planned for you . . . I have good plans for you. I don't plan to hurt you. I plan to give you hope and a good future" (Jer. 29:11).

Because these characteristics can result from other sources besides sexual abuse, don't immediately start accusing people. If you suspect your friend is being abused, find an appropriate situation and ask him or her. If she is being abused then be ready to help by guiding her to authorities. You can't save her yourself. You have to get help from experts and people with the authority to take action to help the victim and stop the abuser (*Youth-worker Journal*, Winter 1985).

Q. *One of my friends has been sexually abused. How can I help?*

A. Serving as a support person will help your friend more than anything else. Much of the pain a victim experiences comes from feeling all alone and that no one understands or wants to help. Having a friend to talk with gives much needed hope and encouragement.

As a support person, your main role is to point your friend in the direction of help. Sexual abuse is one of the most difficult experiences to overcome. There are professional Christian counselors trained to deal with this situation. Encourage your hurting friend to see a counselor. Offer to go along.

Q. *Where was God when my sexual abuse happened?*

A. God never calls evil good. He was not the one who orchestrated the abuse in your life. It is because of human sinfulness that these tragic events occur. It is also because Satan desires to "steal and kill and destroy" (John 10:10). Praise God that He is a God of redemption and healing. He is able to redeem anything when we yield it into His loving hands.

God is not the One who caused it, but He is the One who can take care of it. Jesus came to "bind up the brokenhearted and to set at liberty the captives" (see Luke 4:18). He wants to do that in your life. In Ezekiel 36:34–36 God promises, "The desolate land will be cultivated instead of lying desolate in the sight of all who pass through it. They will say, 'This land that was laid waste has become like the garden of Eden; the cities that were lying in ruins, desolate and destroyed, are now fortified and inhabited. Then the nations around you that remain will know that I the LORD have rebuilt what was destroyed and have replanted what was desolate. I the LORD have spoken, and I will do it'" (Jan Frank, *Door of Hope*, HLP, 1987).

Q. How common is physical abuse?

A. Too common. In 1986, more than 2,000,000 cases of child abuse were reported to authorities, compared with 669,000 in 1976. More than 1,200 children die each year through abuse and neglect. And at least 40 percent of all abuse cases involve alcohol or drugs.

"Although child abuse cuts across all economic classes, urban areas are at the highest risk. Under the stress of single parenting, parents are more likely to strike their children. Parents who were themselves abused as children are six times more likely to mistreat their own children" (*Newsweek* 12/12/88, p. 59).

Q. What are the signs of physical abuse?

A. Here are some signs you should look for if you suspect something is wrong with someone you know:

Unexplained bruises, welts, burns, or broken bones. Everyone gets bruises in the course of growing up, especially in playing sports. But if you notice that someone always has bruises, or has bruises that don't go away, or is very self-conscious of the marks, take note.

Torn or bloody underwear. This primarily has to do with sexual abuse, but torn clothing can also indicate violent struggles between the victim and the abuser.

Abrupt changes in behavior. If someone you know who was laid back starts acting violent, or if she was energetic and now is passive, or if he jumps from mood to mood to mood, this can indicate the person's emotional reactions to abuse.

A desperate desire to please others. An abused person can believe that he or she is to blame for the abuse, because an abuser often screams this at the victim. As a result, the victim may think that if he or she is just nicer or does things better, then the abuse will stop.

Sudden drop in class grades. Apathy can set in and be a factor. Also, think of the tremendous mental burden of being abused but thinking you couldn't tell anyone. In light of that, school just doesn't seem that important.

Suicide attempts. Anyone attempting suicide is usually screaming for help. Always pay attention to someone who is either attempting or threatening suicide (*Newsweek* 12/12/88, p. 61).

Q. What effect does physical abuse have on someone?

A. Abuse rips at a person's sense of worth and dignity. Abuse can destroy his or her faith in God. At its worst, abuse can take the victim's life.

Listen to one woman's testimony:

> "To him it was a bad experience. To me, it was a loss of self. He regrets, then forgets. I will never forget.
>
> "I don't have a single broken bone. The only remains of the experience are those which none can see, scars which affect me in the way I feel more alone than ever.
>
> "It hurts to be hit. It hurts to have someone look at you with eyes that see so little and with hands that exercise no restraint.

"Long after the action, when those eyes are no longer looking at you, there still remains an imprint deep in your soul as you begin to look at yourself as those eyes did.

"All of a sudden, no matter where you stood before, you become as small as you were to those eyes which saw you in the heat of anger.

"The loss of self-respect is immense.

"Nobody should be hit. Not an animal, not a man, not a woman, nor a child. Nothing beautiful should be made to feel less than something that deserves respect.

"I feel like I have been robbed of the beauty I saw in myself" (Lewis Grizzard, Syndicated Column).

Q. What is the difference between discipline and physical abuse?

A. To distinguish between discipline and abuse, the first place to look is the intended result of the action. Someone who is trying to discipline his or her child is acting out of love in the best interest of the child. Abuse is intended to make the child feel pain, and it rises not out of love or desire to help but out of anger.

However, some abusers will tell the victim that the abuse is "for your own good," or "to teach you a lesson." So the next place to look is the physical and emotional result. *Discipline should not leave any physical or emotional scars.*

After that, you can look at the relationship between the victim and the abuser. Loving discipline draws the two together, creating a better, less tense, more understanding relationship. Abuse pushes the two apart—as does violence between any two people.

In general, discipline is loving, with no physical or emotional harm, and creates a better relationship. Abuse is destructive, evil, and tears apart relationships.

Q. How do I get help? How do I help a friend who's being physically abused?

A. If you're being abused, you have to get out! Until an abuser is forced to confront his crime, he won't stop. The first step of action is to protect yourself and get away from the abuser.

Most state child welfare agencies have a hot-line number that you can call. Look in your local phone book under the "State Government" section for the number. Also, there is a national referral service at a toll-free number that can guide you to help. This call doesn't cost you anything, 800-4-A-CHILD (800-422-4453).

If your situation is an emergency, call the police. Most areas now have 911 emergency numbers. Try this first. If it doesn't work in your area, look up the police number in the front of your phone book or under the local government section.

You are a child of God whom He has created with dignity and worth. Don't let an abuser try to strip you of that worth and dignity. Get help, now (*Newsweek* 12/12/88, p. 61).

Selected Bibliography

Baucom, John Q., *Help Your Children Say No to Drugs*, Grand Rapids, MI: Zondervan Publishing House, 1987.

Campolo, Anthony, "Breaking Out of the Dating Game," *A Straight Word to Kids and Parents*, New York: Plough Publishing House, 1987.

Frank, Jan, *Door of Hope*, San Bernardino, CA: Here's Life Publishers, 1987.

Grizzard, Lewis, "Hits That Hurt," *Atlanta Journal and Constitution*, 1988.

Hunt, Gary and Angela, *Mom & Dad Don't Live Together Anymore*, San Bernardino, CA: Here's Life Publishers, 1989.

Jones, William H., *Parents: Raising Them Properly*, San Bernardino, CA: Here's Life Publishers, 1988.

————, *Self-Image: Learning to Like Yourself*, San Bernardino, CA: Here's Life Publishers, 1988.

————, *Temptation: Avoiding the Big Rip-Off*, San Bernardino, CA: Here's Life Publishers, 1988.

————, *Peer Pressure: Standing Up for What You Believe*, San Bernardino, CA: Here's Life Publishers, 1988.

————, *Friendships: Making the Best of Them*, San Bernardino, CA: Here's Life Publishers, 1989.

McDowell, Josh, *His Image. . .My Image*, San Bernardino, CA: Here's Life Publishers, 1984.

————, & Day, Dick, *Why Wait?*, San Bernardino, CA: Here's Life Publishers, 1987.

Myers, Bill, *More Hot Topics*, Wheaton, IL: Victor Books, 1989.

St. Clair, Barry & Jones, William H., *Love: Making It Last*, San Bernardino, CA: Here's Life Publishers, 1988.

————, *Dating: Picking (and Being) a Winner*, San Bernardino, CA: Here's Life Publishers, 1987.

————, *Sex: Desiring the Best*, San Bernardino, CA: Here's Life Publishers, 1987.

LET'S STAY -IN- TOUCH!

If you have grown personally as a result of this material, we should stay in touch. You will want to continue in your Christian growth, and to help your faith become even stronger, our team is constantly developing new materials.

We are now publishing a monthly newsletter called <u>5 Minutes with Josh</u> which will

1) tell you about those new materials as they become available
2) answer your tough questions
3) give creative tips on being an effective parent
4) let you know our ministry needs
5) keep you up to date on my speaking schedule (so you can pray).

If you would like to receive this publication, simply fill out the coupon below and send it in. By special arrangement <u>5 Minutes with Josh</u> will come to you regularly — <u>no charge</u>.

Let's keep in touch!

Josh

☐ **Yes!** I want to receive the free subscription to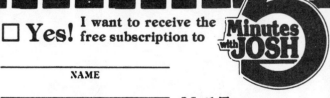

NAME

ADDRESS

CITY, STATE/ZIP

Mail To:
Josh McDowell
c/o <u>5 Minutes with Josh</u>
Campus Crusade for Christ
Arrowhead Springs
San Bernardino, CA 92414

SLC-2024

BOOKS

How to Help Your Child Say "No"		
to Sexual Pressure	tp	084-9930-936
Love, Dad	tp	084-9931-274
Unlocking the Secrets of Being		
Loved, Accepted, and Secure 🖎	tp	084-9931-711

AUDIO

How to Help Your Child Say "No"		
to Sexual Pressure	HTLsc	201-0837-002
"No!"—The Positive Answer		
(Love Waiting Music)	sc	201-9302-713
The Secret of Loving	LLsc	201-0168-712
The Teenage Q&A Book on Tape	BTca	084-9912-644
Why Wait?: What You Need to Know		
About the Teen Sexuality Crisis ➡	BTca	084-9912-814
Why Waiting is Worth the Wait	LLsc	084-9912-512

VIDEOS AND VIDEO CURRICULUM

A Clean Heart for a New Start	vc	084-9911-117
Evidence for Faith	vcr	801-9100-792
God Is No Cosmic Kill-Joy	vc	084-9911-095
How to Handle the Pressure Lines	vc	084-9911-125
How to Help Your Child Say "No"		
to Sexual Pressure	vcr	801-8900-795
Let's Talk About Love and Sex	vcr	801-5060-796
The Myths of Sex Education	vc	084-9911-133
"No!"—The Positive Answer	vcr	801-9300-791
The Teenage Q&A Video Series	vcr	084-9911-575
Where Youth Are Today	vc	801-3591-794
Who Do You Listen To?	vc	084-9911-141
Why Waiting Is Worth the Wait	vc	084-9911-109

FILMS

Evidence for Faith Series:
    Messianic Prophecy
    Misconceptions about Christianity, Part I
    Misconceptions about Christianity, Part II
    The Reliability of Scripture
    A Skeptic's Quest
    The Uniqueness of the Bible
Where Youth are Today: What You Need to Know about the
    Teen Sexuality Crisis

✍ Co-authored with Dale Bellis
✆ Co-authored with Dick Day

KEY TO PRODUCT TYPE

BTca   BookTrax cassette album
HTLsc How-To Library audio cassette
LLsc   Life Lifter audio cassette
vc   video cassette
vcr   video curriculum resource
sc   single cassette
tp   trade paper book